# Harley James & the Secret of the Falcon Queen

## Leah Cupps

Copyright © 2022 Leah Cupps & Vision Forty Press

Harley James Adventures® is a Trademark of Leah Cupps.

www.HarleyJamesAdventures.com

All rights reserved.

No part of this book may be reproduced in any form or by any electronic or mechanical means, including information storage and retrieval systems, without written permission from the author, except for the use of brief quotations in a book review.

ISBN: 978-1-7344055-5-2

NOTE: While inspired by real events, this is a work of fiction and does not claim to be historically accurate or portray factual events or relationships. References to historical events, real persons, business establishments and real places are used fictitiously and my not be factually accurate, but rather fictionalized by the author.

*Dedicated to my daughter, Savannah Cupps.*

*Her curiosity, adventurous spirit and love of dogs inspired the Harley James books.*

# FREE ACTIVITY KIT

Dear Friend,

Welcome! My name is Harley James and this is my story, the Secret of the Falcon Queen. I'm so glad you're here!

If you love riddles and puzzles as much as I do, then you must download the free activity kit I made, just for you! It includes mazes, puzzles and of course, secret messages!

Go to HarleyJamesAdventures.com to download this fun activity kit for free!

Until then, Happy Reading!

*Harley James*

P.S. Some of the characters & history in this story is fictional, and some is true. Want to know what's what?

Go to HarleyJamesAdventures.com and click on our free Fact or Fiction Video Series to find out more.

www.HarleyJamesAdventures.com

# CONTENTS

| | |
|---|---:|
| Prologue | 1 |
| 1. The Silver Feather | 7 |
| 2. The Legend of the Falcon Queen | 14 |
| 3. Kirks Are for Kings | 24 |
| 4. Don't Mess with Magnus Murdoch | 31 |
| 5. Meeting at Midnight | 37 |
| 6. A Horse's Tale | 46 |
| 7. The Pickle of the Pictish Runes | 58 |
| 8. Bagpipes Over the Mountains | 63 |
| 9. Scavenger Hunt | 70 |
| 10. The Great Chase | 76 |
| 11. Waterfall by the Sea | 79 |
| 12. A Secret Chamber | 84 |
| 13. Mountains of Muckle | 90 |
| 14. Grounded | 94 |
| 15. A Leap of Faith | 98 |
| 16. Down the Cellars We Go | 103 |
| 17. Who Can You Trust? | 108 |
| 18. Book of Spells | 113 |
| 19. Betrayal | 117 |
| 20. No Way Out | 121 |
| 21. Fireworks | 126 |
| 22. Water Kelpie | 129 |
| 23. The Fountain of Fireworks | 134 |
| 24. Never Say Goodbye | 139 |
| About the Author | 143 |

# PROLOGUE

*A*round *600 years ago in a Scottish Castle.*
Queen Catherine ran down the castle hall, holding her skirts up to move as fast as she possibly could. Her slippers were silent on the heavy stones. Long, red hair flowed behind her as she followed the torchlight. She only had a few moments before her servants noticed she was gone.

She had to hide the book. It must not fall into the wrong hands, or disaster would surely follow.

She knew what the townspeople thought of her and the leather-bound book she always kept at her side. Many said that it contained spells and sorcery. Some believed it held the ability to raise the dead between its bejeweled covers.

There were those who said the queen's book once belonged to the legendary wizard Merlin himself. Others claimed it was simply filled with state secrets. And still more believed it gave the queen the power to control minds, especially that of their king.

Only the queen knew its true power. Regardless, countless

people would have loved to get their hands on it. Of that there was no doubt.

As queen of this part of the Highlands, Catherine was rarely left alone, always surrounded by her handmaidens. This evening she saw an opportunity to sneak off while everyone was at the banquet. She pushed aside a tapestry and darted down the hidden steps, sure that she had enough time to hide her treasure. She knew she should probably destroy it, for the power it held inside, but she couldn't bear to.

The contents were nobody's business but her own. She did not have to answer to anyone. But if the townspeople made enough noise, they could sway the court's thinking and eventually that of her husband, the king.

He had always been suspicious of her treasured book. But he looked the other way, afraid of angering her. The court was beginning to talk, however. The king's advisors were starting to question her activities and soon he would have to do something. She knew he wouldn't ignore it much longer.

She had to find some place to conceal her book before the prying eyes of the public got hold of it. She ran deeper through the tunnels, looking for the perfect hiding spot.

Finally she found it. She quickly wrapped the journal in linens and laid it in a place where no one would ever think to look. She bowed her head and took a long breath.

The words of the spell came to her easily. She kept her voice to a whisper. Stones began to move and the sound of jingling keys floated down the tunnel.

When it was done, she darted back through the tunnels and emerged into the night. The unmistakable, high-pitched cry of a falcon pierced the silence of the night.

*My dear falcon.*

The villagers swore she could speak to the bird and see

through its eyes. Many suspected she had an improper bond with the falconer who kept the crown's birds. But her loyalty lay with the king, the one man she loved. She glanced up to see her raptor circling in the sky. The bird was off to do his work and deliver a message.

A message she hoped would make it to the king, before it was too late.

## CHAPTER 1
# THE SILVER FEATHER

It was the eyes that caught my attention. They were mesmerizing. I stared at the portrait. A red-haired woman looked down at me with a piercing gaze. It was an antique oil painting, but it looked so lifelike. I took several steps to my left. The eyes followed. I skipped over to the right. The woman's pale green eyes seemed to move with me.

*How is that possible?*

She was dressed in an elaborate gown and wore a golden circlet around her scarlet hair. With her robes and her jeweled crown, she looked like a queen ready for court. She stood on the veranda, next to a spouting water fountain with a stone horse emerging from its center. A tall bird sat on her wrist, its talons clinging to a thick leather gauntlet. I stood for several moments, captivated by the image.

My dog, Daisy, stared up at the bird. We were exploring the hallways of an eight-hundred-year-old castle nestled in the Isle of the Skye in Scotland. My fuzzy little pooch tilted her head slightly to one side with that comical look she got when she was confused.

"It's okay, girl," I said. "It's just a picture."

Still, there was something about it. The portrait was in one of those heavy gold frames that screamed old money. In the background was the castle with the loch in the distance.

"Lovely, isn't she?" I heard an heavily accented voice behind me.

I turned to find a heavyset older man standing there. He had on a vest with a pocket watch, and a tweed cap rested atop his head.

"Yes, sir, she is," I said.

"Catherine was once the queen of Dunvegan Castle," said the gentleman, waving his hand in a circle. "Known throughout the Highlands for her grace and beauty. Are you here for the tour?"

"Oh, no, I'm here with my dad. He's an archaeologist."

"Wouldn't be Russell James, would it?"

"As a matter of fact…"

"Quite, quite. Your father is famous, too."

"I guess…"

"Everyone's been in a tizzy since he arrived. I've heard he's been hired by Magnus Murdoch to excavate the king's tomb. Quite an honor."

"That's right," I said, tucking a strand of hair behind my ear. "He gets to do all kinds of honorable things."

"Aye." The man looked down at me and Daisy. "Please, please pardon me, how rude of me. I'm Callum McKenzie, a tour guide here, among other things." He extended a chubby hand which I shook.

"I'm Harley James. This is Daisy."

"Pleased to meet you, Miss James." Mr. McKenzie touched the brim of his hat and bowed his head slightly. "I work for the estate. If you have any questions or any needs, by all means seek me out."

Mr. McKenzie turned to go. A mother and daughter stepped toward the portrait and started to chat beside me.

"I do have one question..." I said, pointing at the queen.

Mr. McKenzie tilted his head to the side, as if to say, go ahead. He looked a bit like Daisy when she was befuddled.

"Why the bird?"

"Oh, yes, yes, Queen Catherine was known for her prized merlin—that's a kind of falcon—and seemed to have an almost mystical connection with it. Some of the villagers even referred to it as her familiar."

"Sorry, I'm not familiar... with... that term," I said, trying not to smile at my amazing pun.

"Clever, you are, I see what you did there. Yes, well, a familiar was said to be the spirit animal of a witch or magician."

"The queen was a witch?" I said this maybe a little too loud, and my voice echoed off the castle's stone. The mother and daughter turned to look at me.

"So the rumors say. Of course, that was a long time ago when many people did not benefit from proper education."

My phone beeped then, and just when the conversation was getting interesting.

*A witch?*

I glanced at the phone. If I didn't respond, I'd end up grounded and stuck in my room for days.

"Excuse me, Mr. McKenzie, that's my dad."

"Yes, yes, very nice to meet you, Miss James. I hope you enjoy your time in Scotland. Oh, and Miss James?"

"Yes?"

"I was asked to give you this." Mr. McKenzie handed me a large, business-size envelope.

"Thanks," I said. I turned the envelope over in my hand.

"Miss James?"

"Yes?"

"Don't open that here."

I nodded and walked off. *That was odd.*

I stepped over to the wall and swiped open my phone. My dad had texted me twice. He wanted me to meet him at the dig site. I texted him back: *On my way.*

"Come on, Daisy," I said. She looked up at me and gave a quick wag of the tail.

We started back the way we came. As we walked past a tapestry, it ruffled in a breeze coming from somewhere within the keep.

These old castles sure were drafty.

I paused for a moment, tempted to break the seal on the envelope. Next to me, Daisy stopped. Her ears stood up, moving like big satellite dishes to home in on a sound. Then she bolted down the hallway, her nails ticking away on the hard stone.

"Daisy!" I hollered after her. She didn't pause for a second.

I chased deeper into the castle, following her barking. I barely spotted her tail zip around a corner, and then she was gone. When I jogged up to that point, though, there was no corner—just a solid mass of granite stones.

A huge tapestry hung on the wall, depicting a landscape scene. It showed the castle towering above the countryside, falcons flying through a blue sky, and a group of knights on horses riding through a meadow.

I walked past the tapestry, looking for any doors or hallways. Nothing.

Was I imagining something?

I could still hear Daisy barking. She sounded close, but where was she?

I yelled, "Daisy!"

The barking stopped. And then the tapestry moved, and there she was, wagging her tail. Her big eyes looked up at me.

"Where were you?" I said, pulling the huge cloth back like a curtain. She must have been chasing a mouse.

I gasped. Hidden behind the tapestry was a narrow passageway. It was just wide enough that I could walk in without turning sideways. There was a step up to get into it, and I couldn't see more than a few feet because it was so dark. I switched my phone flashlight on and cast the light ahead.

*A secret hallway.*

Behind me, I heard voices, followed by heels clicking on the castle's stone. I stepped into the passage, motioning Daisy to follow. I let go of the tapestry and leaned up against the wall. The tapestry waved, but the voices traveled on past, apparently not noticing.

Once they were gone, I walked deeper into the secret space. I found myself in a big, open chamber. I turned off my tiny phone light and pulled a flashlight out of my backpack for a closer look around.

It seemed as if I had discovered a secret room.

Old, moldy rugs covered the floor, and cobwebs were draped across a heavy wood desk and a big chair. Beside them was a bucket with water in it. She stared at it for a moment, wondering why the water had no evaporated after all these years.

More tapestries hung from the walls. I stepped over and scanned them with the flashlight. One showed a family crest—a shield with a falcon in one corner and a stag in the other. I assumed this was the symbol of the king and queen of the castle. I'd seen it a couple places already. On another was a picture of the red-haired Queen Catherine on a horse in a moonlit forest. She was dressed in a gold-colored gown, had a falcon on her arm, and rode toward the loch.

*She really likes these birds.*

As I took in the room, my eyes landed on a strange board on the opposite wall. On it a series of keys hung neatly in rows. In the center of them was a keyhole. Above the display was a two-line poem:

*A Horse with Nee Legs,*
*She Rides in Night*
*Protect Ye Spirit From Her,*
*or Drown You She Might.*

"Oooh, Daisy, a riddle." Riddles were my specialty. I love any sort of mind games. I'm a bit of an amateur cryptologist. Solving puzzles and secret codes has become one of my trademarks skills.

*A horse with no legs, She rides in night.*

Hmmm. I looked at the big tapestry. The queen was riding at night, but her stallion had all four legs.

A no-legged horse.

Minus four?

I looked at the board and counted four hooks to the left of the keyhole. I picked the dusty skeleton key off its perch. It had an image of a horse emerging from the loch on it.

*A horse with no legs.*

I placed it in the lock and turned. It made a click. But nothing opened.

I thought some more.

*Rides at night.*

I looked to see if any of the other keys had designs. One in the top row had a moon on it. I pushed up on my tippy-toes to reach it.

I placed that one in the lock. The key turned farther than the last one and I heard another click. But nothing opened.

*Drown you, she might.*

I kept searching and found another key with an engraving that looked like a triangle of waves. I placed that one in the lock. Now I had all three keys and their symbols...a horse with no legs, a moon, and the symbol for water.

I held my breath as I placed the third key in the lock and rotated it. This time it turned all the way around, made a tell-tale click, and a tiny slot opened.

Inside was an object wrapped in green velvet cloth. I pulled it out, and a silver feather fell into my hands. I looked at it in awe. The beautiful detail was so lifelike. The feather was long as a bookmark and made of some sort of metal.

My phone beeped loudly, the sound bouncing off the walls of the secret room. I scrambled to turn off the volume and nearly dropped the feather to the floor.

*Crap, Dad is waiting!*

I opened my messages. He'd sent me multiple texts.

> *Harley, where have you disappeared to?*
> *My laptop's been stolen!*
> *I need you to hurry out to the dig site.*
> *I have a ride waiting for you outside the castle.*

Dad's laptop was stolen? I tucked my newly found feather and the envelope into my purple backpack.

Unfortunately, my curiosity would have to wait.

## CHAPTER 2
# THE LEGEND OF THE FALCON QUEEN

I hurried out from behind the tapestry and darted outside. After the darkness of the castle, it took my eyes some time to adjust to the bright sky. Daisy and I stepped into an open clearing dominated by a big water fountain. It had the same horse emerging from the center as the one in the portrait.

The keep had a dramatic view of the loch, with sweeping meadows down to the water. The land made rolling, grassy waves, and the loch itself looked as big as the ocean. I could see why they decided to build a castle right here.

"This is my kind of place, Daisy," I said, kneeling to give her a hug. She licked my face and nuzzled my ear. Daisy and I were tight, having been through a lot. We'd stared down tomb raiders in Guatemala and braved the massive seas of a hurricane in Jamaica, almost drowning together.

I don't know what I'd do without her.

"Queen Catherine had this fountain built herself," I heard a young voice say.

I looked up to see a pair of knobby knees. I raised my head

further to discover the knees belonged to a dark-haired boy who looked to be about my age. He was wearing shorts, sneakers, and a green and white long-sleeve T-shirt.

"It's beautiful," I said as I stood up.

"You must be Harley?" His deep blue eyes stared at me quizzically.

"That's me," I said. "And this is Daisy."

The boy took a knee to pat Daisy. "I'm Remington Reid," he said, scratching Daisy behind her ears. "Most people call me Remi. My dad is the manager of this place. He told me you would be visiting."

"You live right here, then?"

"Yeah. My family have been in this castle for centuries."

"Wow, that's neat. I'd love to live here."

"Pure dead brilliant," he said, almost grumbling as he spoke.

"What's that mean?"

"Sorry, I forgot you Yanks aren't familiar with Scottish slang. Means amazing, or really great. But I was being sarcastic."

"You don't like it here?"

He shrugged.

"It's okay. I guess. I get bored a lot of the time. Wi-Fi isn't great surrounded by all this granite, and there's usually no kids around."

"I get that. I travel all the time with my dad. Everyone assumes it must be awesome, but sometimes I wish I had a house and a yard, a school, and a soccer team. Just be a kid."

"Mmm. Soccer? You mean footie?"

"Yes, footie. Right," I said, feeling the heat rise in my cheeks. It was going to take me a minute to get the hang of the language.

"Remi!" A voice interrupted our conversation. It came from off to my right. I shaded my eyes against the sun and looked over. A girl with a shock of blazing hair—the color of a fresh carrot—

was beckoning us over from a driveway. She stood beside a dark green Range Rover.

"That's my sister, Freya."

"We leave in five minutes," she shouted. "Did you get everything I asked for?"

"Just a moment!" Remi replied. He looked back at me. "Give me a few minutes, and we'll head out."

"Head out to where?"

"We're supposed to pick you up and take you to the dig site." He nodded in the direction of the Range Rover, where they were loading up large coolers. "We're bringing the lunch to the team."

"Oh, right," I said. Dad had mentioned a ride. "I'll wait here."

Remi trotted off toward the castle, and I looked around. It appeared I was alone. This was a better time than any to open the envelope I received.

I leaned up against a nearby tree and tore open the envelope. Inside was a letter folded into thirds. I pulled it out and tried to flatten it as best as I could.

I squinted in the sunlight to read it, but found that it was handwritten gibberish.

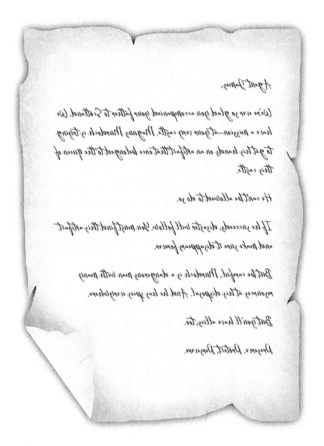

*Great.*

I looked closer. It looked as if the letter was written…backwards.

*Mirror writing!*

Mirror writing was a common way to code messages. The letters were written backwards and nearly impossible to decipher. But hold them in front of a mirror and they were easy to read.

Which meant I needed to find a mirror as soon as possible.

"Remi?" I called as I saw the boy emerge from around the corner. "Is there a bathroom nearby?"

"Looking for the loo, eh? It's just around that corner." He

pointed to a side entrance to the castle. "But be quick about it, we leave in a just a moment."

I nodded and hurried toward the castle. After I had carefully locked the door to the loo—as Remi called it—I pulled out the letter and held it in front of the mirror. Just as I had predicted, the words became clear.

*Agent James,*
*We're ever so glad you accompanied your father to Scotland. We have a mission—at your very castle. Magnus Murdoch is trying to get his hands on an artifact that once belonged to the queen of this castle.*

*He can't be allowed to do so.*

*If he succeeds, disaster will follow. You must find this artifact and make sure it disappears forever.*

*But be careful, Murdoch is a dangerous man with many resources at his disposal. And he has spies everywhere.*
*But you'll have allies, too.*

*Preserve. Protect. Persevere.*

I shifted the letter in the light that poured in through the window and caught the faint symbol of S.M.A.L.L., an owl with a half-moon on its head and an arrow in its clutches.

I heard a few shouts from outside. It was time to go. I stashed the letter in my backpack, carefully folding it closed.

My mind was buzzing with ideas as I strode toward the waiting caravan of Rovers.

The silver feather I had found, the secret message from S.M.A.L.L., and the fact that someone had stolen my dad's laptop. What did it all mean? I hoped the car ride to the loch would give me some time to think it through.

Unfortunately, my hope was in vain.

WE BUMPED along a dirt road through a forest of old oak and birch trees, with the occasional pine sprinkled in. Freya was in the front with the driver, but she kept turning around to ask me questions.

Daisy sat between Remi and me in the back. She seemed content. The whole car smelled like ham, and she was happy to go anywhere with food.

"Your sister seems really cool," I whispered to Remi, who rolled his eyes and looked out the window.

*Sibling rivalry?* I'd always heard siblings fought a lot, but seeing as how I didn't have one, I'd never know firsthand.

The countryside was lovely, and I imagined knights galloping through the woods and archers in green camouflaged in the leaves.

*You've seen too many movies,* I told myself.

Then I remembered the picture of the queen I'd seen riding in similar country. I wondered if Freya and Remi shared any of her blood. Freya and the queen even had the same flaming hair.

I turned to Remi. "Is it true that Queen Catherine was a witch?"

"Some say, I dinnae ken for sure."

"Dinner ken?"

He chuckled. "It means I don't know."

"Ah."

When I was in Jamaica last year, I really enjoyed listening to the locals talk. Same was true in Scotland, but Remi spoke like he was talking with marbles in his mouth. I made a mental note to Google Scottish slang when I arrived back to my room.

"But that was what the locals said, right?"

"Many of them, yes. Could be that she was simply an herbalist or maybe even a scientist. Superstitious lot back then."

"What happened to her?"

"Long story, that. Legend goes that the villagers were afraid of her. And her diary, which they believed was full of spells. When the king was traveling, they threatened to burn her out of the castle. She sped off into the woods to hide and sent a falcon to the king with a note begging him to return and protect her. He never came. The townspeople caught her and told her she had to give up her book of spells or they'd kill her. She refused, and they drowned her in the lake."

"Wow. That is some story."

Remi patted Daisy, and she nuzzled him in return. "I guess it's mostly true. They say her body was found the next day by her falcon. Then it flew off and never returned."

"What did the king do?"

"He was crushed. He had thought she was being dramatic and was in no real danger. He'd left several men from his guard to protect her. But they were afraid of her, too, and stepped aside when the villagers came for her. He abandoned the castle and went into seclusion. It was empty for centuries."

"Really? It looks to be in great shape."

"Several years ago, a billionaire named Magnus Murdoch bought it. That's who my dad works for. He invested a lot of money restoring the castle, hired staff, and opened it to tourists."

"What's in it for him? I mean, I doubt that enough visitors come by to pay for all the upkeep needed." I petted Daisy, who was watching intently out the window.

"True," he said. Then he brushed a bit of black hair from his forehead and leaned toward me. "They say the dig was set up to unearth Scottish artifacts, but he really wants the queen's diary. Historians see it as a rare treasure, covered in jewels. But there is a group of people who believe it has special powers." He lowered his voice to a whisper. "Like the wizard Merlin and all that."

My thoughts instantly went to the mysterious letter I had just received from S.M.A.L.L.

"What kind of powers?"

Remi shrugged. "The villagers believed the queen used it to control the king's mind. Either way, Mr. Murdoch has been trying to get his hands on it."

"But he hasn't found it yet?" I asked.

He shook his head. "Not yet."

A chill ran through me. But I didn't want to say anything to Remi—at least not yet.

# CHAPTER 3
# KIRKS ARE FOR KINGS

**U**ggh. Boats.
My stomach had that awful feeling again. Like the bottom of it was going to the top, and the top was dropping to the bottom.

*I hate boats.*

I looked out across the loch. We had loaded lunch into our boat and were now speeding across the black surface. The water was choppy, causing our small speedboat to bounce up and down like a carnival ride.

I learned a few tricks to combat seasickness when I was in Jamaica, but none were working now. I couldn't go to the middle of the boat because it was super small, with barely enough room for the four of us and Daisy. I couldn't look at the distant horizon —there was an island blocking the view.

So, I had to sit and try to breathe. The mist coming off the loch at least felt good against my face. It was cool in the spring sun and the small island up ahead was getting closer.

*Thankfully, we don't have far to go.*

"You're awfully quiet, Harley," Remi said.

I clenched my hands into fists. "Just trying not to throw up."

"Ah. It gives me the boke, as well."

"Boke?"

"Sickness."

I added *boke* to my mental list of Scottish words I should know.

Luckily for me, the boat throttled down just then, coasting up to the dock. It was a short crossing, but even so, I was glad to stand on the solid steel of the pier. It didn't move or sway or buckle or rock in any way. My legs continued to shake, and I knew it would take a while for my balance to return.

"This way, Harley." Remi pointed up across a broad lawn at a wide forest path. Four golf carts appeared out of the woods and drove down toward us. As the carts grew closer, I got a good look at them. With their giant off-road tires, they looked more like miniature monster trucks than golf carts. The drivers had on matching khaki tops and bottoms.

It all felt oddly fancy for an archaeological dig site.

"I've been to a lot of digs with my dad," I said to Freya, "but I've never seen hot rods like these. On most sites the golf carts look as antique as the artifacts. And uniforms, no less," I added as I pointed to the drivers.

Freya smiled. "Wait until you see the pits."

"Hello, Ms. Reid," said one of the archaeologists. Freya nodded with confidence. Clearly she was in charge.

"Do you come out to the dig site often?" I asked her.

"I do a lot of errands for Mr. Murdoch. Sort of a gopher," Freya said.

*So, she is Murdoch's right-hand man?* That can't be good. Maybe she doesn't know what her boss is up to.

While the archaeologists loaded the golf carts with the cooler,

Remi, Freya, and I left the waving grasses of the shore and headed up the trail. The woods wrapped their leafy arms around us. Everything was green—emerald moss covered the ground as far as the eyes could see and pine trees soared above us.

Daisy bobbed along the trail next to me, sniffing everything in sight. I thought about the letter from S.M.A.L.L. and the queen's diary.

*Could it really be magical?*

I wouldn't have believed that sort of stuff a few years ago, but after my adventures in the Mayan ruins and the sunken pirate city, I was a bit more open-minded.

After a short walk, the trees gave way to a clearing filled with people and movement. Boardwalks went every which way around a crumbling stone building. Only one wall remained upright—a rectangle with the triangle at the top—and it had a large, graceful arched window opening halfway up. Around it the other walls lay on the ground in piles. Moss grew up and over many of the stones.

Freya leaned down to pet Daisy and said, "I have to go see to some things. Stay out of trouble, you two."

Remi and I continued walking on the boardwalk that went around the site. Nearby, archaeologists crouched in shallow pits, big brown holes laid out in a grid. In addition to the boardwalks, there were high-tech computer stations and big-walled tents and light towers and solar arrays. It looked more like movie set than a dig.

"This is the kirk," said Remi. "Where King Robert was buried. Most of the Scottish kings were buried in big abbeys, but Robert wanted to be near his wife, Catherine, so instead he's here in this tomb."

"Kirk?"

"It's another word for church or chapel."

I added it to the growing list in my mind and decided I was going to have to start writing it down in my journal.

I walked along behind Daisy, who was introducing herself to everyone she met. This was done with licks, tail wagging, and even a handful of belly rubs. She loved people and was shameless.

I'd never been to a fancier dig in my life. One archaeologist was being followed around by a young woman taking down his notes, like he was the boss of a major corporation. A man in a dark shirt and jacket and even darker slacks stood off to one side. Even though the sun was hardly visible behind the trees, he wore sunglasses. He just stood there watching, his hands clasped in front of him.

"This is unbelievable," I said to Remi. "Most of the archaeology sites I've ever been to were just a few people scraping at the dirt. You know, low budget. College kids and a few paid staff. These archaeologists have *assistants*. And who's that guy?" I nodded toward the man in black, who was looking in our direction.

"Mr. Murdoch spares no expense." Remi shrugged. "And that's one of the men in Murdoch's security detail."

"Security detail? At an archaeological site? Really?"

"I guess the thinking is if they find something valuable—which is the whole point of the dig—he doesn't want it going anywhere."

The man in black continued to stare our way, as if two kids were a major threat, here to pilfer and plunder like Vikings.

A voice blared over a loudspeaker. "Lunch is served in the pavilion."

"Well, that was quick," I said to Remi.

"I think it was just fancy sandwiches."

*Fancy sandwiches.*

Remi started to walk toward the pavilion.

"I'm not hungry," I said. "I want to have a look around."

"Suit yourself," Remi said, without turning around.

I followed the boardwalk toward the lone standing wall. The pits were pristine, with little retaining walls in place and perfect ninety-degree corners. The sifting tables were motorized, meaning no one had to sit and shake the dirt through. Lockboxes the size of tiny refrigerators sat next to them on pedestals, presumably to hold the valuable findings. I peeked inside the glass window of one. Several rings sat on cushions.

A deep voice from behind me caused me to jump. "Don't get too close to the artifacts."

I looked back. It was a man dressed all in black, but not the one I'd seen earlier.

*How many of these guys are there?*

"Sorry, just curious."

He was unimpressed. "Who are you and why are you here?"

"See, now you're curious about me."

"Don't be smart. Answer the question."

Taller than the last guy, his sports jacket clinging to his muscles, he was all business, staring down at me. I stared back at him.

"I'm—" I began but was interrupted by someone approaching us.

Daisy stood beside me, not liking the feel of this interchange. She could always sense tension. She looked from me to him and him to me, her little brow furrowed.

"What is going on here?" said a middle-aged man as he stepped toward us. He was also wearing a blazer, with pressed chinos and loafers with tassels. He looked at the guy for answers, ignoring me.

"I caught this girl snooping around the safe."

"I wasn't snooping—"

"Quiet, young lady," said the new guy, turning to me. "Who are you and why are you at my site?"

"I'm Harley James. My father works here."

"Russell James?"

"Yes. I was supposed to meet him. I came with Remi and Freya."

"I see. Why are you not at the lunch?"

"I was more curious than I was hungry."

"Curiosity gets children into trouble."

"Or it helps them grow into intelligent adults," I replied. Dad would probably ground me for speaking to his boss like this, but I couldn't help myself. He just seemed so smug.

"Aren't you the clever one?" the man said. "Just like your father."

I wasn't sure how to take that. Was he suggesting my father was a troublemaker?

"I'm Magnus Murdoch." He extended his hand out to me. "This is my dig. You're staying at my castle."

"Nice to meet you, Mr. Murdoch. I'm Harley James," I said. "And this is my dog, Daisy."

He didn't even look down. Instead he said, "May I show you around? We've already made some interesting discoveries."

"If it's okay with you, I'd like to keep walking around. Remi was just about to show me—"

"No, that's not okay. This is not an open site." Murdoch stared down at me. His small beady eyes straddled a too-small nose. "Follow me, please."

I dropped my shoulders and started off behind him. His goon stepped in behind me.

"As I'm sure your father has told you, this was the tomb of the King of Scots. And not just any king. The Red King whose wife was the enchantress, Queen Catherine."

"Alleged enchantress," I said.

"Excuse me?"

"I've just heard she might also simply have been an herbalist or a scientist. People didn't understand strong women back then."

*Heck, they still don't, but that's not the point here.*

"Hmmm," he said, almost grunting.

*Clearly, he's not interested in my opinions.*

"This is where we found the queen's bracelet," he continued.

I nodded.

"Isn't it extraordinary?" He lifted the wristlet out of the box for me to see. It was made of gold links with deep blue and green jewels wound around it.

I nodded and smiled. It seemed better to keep my mouth shut around Mr. Murdoch.

"We have yet to find the falcon feather, the king's blade, or the kelpie stone. We're also looking for several other items of high interest and exceptional value."

"What sort of items?" I asked, but didn't even listen for an answer.

All I could think about was the first artifact he mentioned. The one nestled in the bottom of the backpack I was wearing.

*The falcon feather.*

## CHAPTER 4
# DON'T MESS WITH MAGNUS MURDOCH

"Hey, Cat-Cat."

I turned to see my dad striding toward us. He was wearing his signature blue field shirt with a red bandana tied around his neck. He brushed a lock of brown hair from his forehead and smiled when he saw me.

*Dad to the rescue.*

"Hey, Dad!" I gave him a big hug.

"Wow. Great to see you, too, kiddo." Dad's enthusiasm was a welcome relief from dour Mr. Murdoch and his henchmen.

"Mr. Murdoch." My dad nodded at Murdoch.

"Mr. James," the boss responded stiffly. "Shouldn't you be digging?"

"Just finished up lunch."

"I see. Well, I must be on my way. I just wanted to get a sense of the day's progress," said Murdoch.

"We're getting there, sir."

"You could get there faster, Russell."

"Doing our best." Dad kept smiling. We stood in silence as Mr. Murdoch stalked away.

"You doing okay, kiddo?" Dad leaned down to look into my eyes.

"Fine, Dad," I said, giving him a reassuring smile. "Did you find your laptop?"

His brows knitted together. "Not yet. I was hoping it'd be here. Or that maybe you borrowed it."

"No, it wasn't me."

"I figured. It was just the weirdest thing. But it will turn up, don't worry. I have my backup at the castle."

I could tell he was trying to reassure me, but something wasn't right. I opened my mouth to ask more questions, but he interrupted.

"Well, I best get back to it, Harley," he said while giving me a squeeze of my shoulders. "Find those other kids. We can't just have you wandering around the dig by yourself."

"Okay, Dad."

I walked toward the wall. Daisy trotted at my heels. On her heels was the towering security guy.

*I guess I have a shadow.*

"Harley." Remi had returned from lunch. "I have something I want to show you."

I rolled my eyes toward the security guy.

"Yeah, it's not on the dig site."

"Okay," I said, eager to get out from under Mr. Murdoch's enforcer.

Remi led me along the boardwalk in the direction of the far side of the island. When we left the walkway, I glanced over my shoulder. The man in the blazer had his hand on his earpiece and was talking. He followed us with his eyes.

"Remi, I've never been to a site like this. It's really weird.

Lockboxes. Security guys tracking your every move. And Mr. Murdoch seemed very suspicious of me, my dad..."

"He's definitely strange. Nobody on the staff likes him. I dinna ken," he said, shrugging his bony shoulders. "I haven't been to other digs, so I'm not sure what normal is."

"This is *so* not normal," I assured him.

Remi led us back into the dense green forest. We hiked along a well-worn path, rust colored from fallen pine needles. It was soft underfoot and the air was cooler when we stepped out of the sun. Tall spruces lofted overhead and everything was still and quiet compared to the bustle and electricity of the dig site.

After about five minutes, the trees gave way to a meadow with the dark waters of the loch behind it. We'd walked clear across the island. At the edge of the field was a three-story stone tower. It stood alone, like a rook from a chess set.

"Pure dead brilliant, isn't it?" Remi said, eyes locked on the tower.

"Say what?"

"Sorry. Cool, huh?" He said this in his idea of an American accent, bobbing his head while he did it.

"It is cool," I replied, ignoring him. "What is it? And why is it here all by itself?"

"We call them follies. Buildings built just for aesthetics."

"It looks kinda sad just sitting there all by itself." The arched windows reminded me of downcast eyes.

"That was the idea. The king had it built after the mob drowned Queen Catherine."

As we got closer, the tower grew taller, and I could see it was perched at the edge of a cliff above the loch. Daisy casually trotted over and looked down. I hung back.

"Daisy, not too close," I called out, like a nervous parent.

Remi and I walked all around the tower. I tiptoed as we got near the precipice.

"There's not even a door," I said.

"Nope. Purely decoration."

On the loch side of the big chess piece was a series of stone carvings. They were about the size of windows, intricately carved, and I recognized the queen in several of them. She was riding a horse in one, sitting by the king on a throne in another, and of course, in each one she had a falcon on her arm. I studied the carvings and noticed there were a few symbols below them. Among them was a feather.

I gasped.

It looked just like the feather I found at the castle. I turned to tell Remi about my discovery. In all the excitement, I'd forgotten to mention it.

But it wasn't Remi who was standing behind me.

"Hello, Harley James. It's been a while."

"Deacon!" I screamed, throwing my arms around his neck. Daisy jumped up on him with her front legs.

"Easy," he said in his trademark British accent. "Good to see you, too, Harley James."

Deacon looked just the same as when I had seen him last, maybe a smidge taller. He had carrot-colored hair and speckles across his pale face. He was wearing his trademark brown fedora, which made him look like a young, red-headed version of Indiana Jones.

"What are you doing here?"

"S.M.A.L.L., of course."

I met Deacon a year ago in Guatemala. He was a special agent working for the Society of Mysterious Artifacts Legends and Lore. We foiled an attempt to steal priceless Mayan statues that, if placed next to one another, would have brought about an apocalypse. After that, he inducted me into S.M.A.L.L. as an agent.

Remi wandered up. He saw Deacon, and to my shock, Remi then pulled a medallion out from under his shirt to show me.

"You're S.M.A.L.L., too?" I couldn't believe it.

Remi nodded. "Preserve. Protect..."

"Persevere," I finished.

"I wanted to tell you but there were always too many people around," he said.

"This dig must be a big deal if they're sending you," I said to Deacon. My mind flashed back to the letter I received. When S.M.A.L.L. mentioned allies, they must have had Deacon in mind. And apparently Remi.

"It is," Deacon said, furrowing his brow. "Murdoch is bad news. He has his stubby fingers searching for all kinds of powerful antiquities. All across the globe. And he really wants the queen's diary. S.M.A.L.L. believes he could use it to control people's minds."

"Really, how?"

"From what I have been told, the diary contains a series of spells. Very old, very powerful. So much so that Queen Catherine went to great lengths to keep it hidden...and out of the wrong hands."

"You mean the queen's diary?"

"That's the one. Murdoch is determined to get a hold of it."

Based on my previous experience with S.M.A.L.L. missions and magical artifacts, I believed what Deacon was saying had to be true.

"Reminds me," I said, reaching into my pack. I learned to carry a pack full of supplies on my expedition to Guatemala.

Never knew what I might need. Sometimes it seemed as if I had the contents of a house in there.

I carefully pulled out the silver feather.

"What's this?" Deacon asked. I told them about the secret room and the puzzle.

"Freya and I found that room," Remi said. "We always thought it was just old storage."

"Storage? There was a puzzle on the wall," I said.

"Yeah, we played with all those keys. Just thought it was some sort of a game. None of the keys worked so we just forgot about it."

"You had to use keys in sequence, and then you got this," I said, pointing at the feather.

"Huh," said Deacon. He looked it over and handed it to Remi, who studied it closely.

"Oh my ..." Remi seemed to lose his voice. After a moment he recovered. "Do you know what this is? This is the falcon feather. It's one of the queen's most famous lost artifacts. This is what they're," he pointed up at the dig site, "all looking for. Legend has it that her friend the falconer used it to send her secret messages." He rolled it in his hands and ran his fingers along the spine. It made a click, and a note slid out of a tiny slot in the side.

It was then that I heard the growl of an engine.

I looked around the tower to see a golf cart with two of Murdoch's henchmen in it. It was coming right at us.

## CHAPTER 5
# MEETING AT MIDNIGHT

The two Murdoch goons stopped the cart almost on Deacon's toes. They stepped out slowly, adjusting their blazers. One had his hand on his earpiece. Neither removed their dark sunglasses. Both were built like football players, and one was taller than the other.

"What are you kids doing?" asked the tall one.

I was behind Remi and furiously trying to put the silver feather back in my pack.

"Looking at the folly, sir," replied Deacon, cool as ever.

"Why?"

"Because we're interested in archaeology."

"Mr. Murdoch doesn't like people taking an interest in his properties."

"We're with the dig, he knows about us," I said, stepping out from behind the boys.

"He knows he doesn't like you kids poking around unsupervised."

*This gets weirder with every second.*

Another golf cart drive up.

"They're with me." Freya climbed out of the cart and came striding toward us, as if she ran the dig and the castle and everything in the nearby vicinity.

"Ms. Reid." The men nodded and stepped back. "Mr. Murdoch doesn't want these kids just walking off wherever they please."

"I'll talk to them. Thanks, guys." Freya gave them a stern look as if to end any argument they might have.

They glared at us and got back into their cart, spinning around and driving back into the woods.

"What *are* you kids doing?" Freya said. "You can't just go poking around the property without an escort. Not with—"

"Kids? Freya, you're only two years older than me," said Remi.

Freya rolled her eyes. "Whatever, Remi."

"What's with all the security?" I asked. "I've been to a zillion dig sites, and I've never seen anything close to this."

"The artifacts rumored to be buried here are quite valuable. Mr. Murdoch is just using due caution."

"Every site has valuable items. I've never seen a special ops force, though."

"Mr. Murdoch just wants to protect his assets. Seems logical to me," said Freya, shrugging. "Anyway, it's time for you to head back to the dig. I can't cover for you all the time."

"Thank you, Freya," Deacon said, extending his hand. "My name's Deacon, by the way."

Freya looked him up and down before taking his hand. "Nice to meet you, Deacon." She gave him a forced smile. "My father mentioned you may be coming. Says you are an old family friend."

Deacon gave her a wide smile. "That's right."

Freya turned on her heel and headed back to her golf cart. She turned her head to face us. "Hop in."

"No thanks," I said. "We'll walk."

"Suit yourselves." She spun her cart around, heading back toward the dig site.

We started walking that way, silent for a few moments.

"That note," I said quietly. "I want to read it. I just want to do it someplace where's Murdoch's men can't see us."

"Wise," said Deacon. "Let's meet again near the castle."

"I know a few places where we won't see Murdoch's goons," Remi said. "The stables, for one. They're not far from the castle and for some reason there's no security cameras there."

"Good idea," said Deacon. "Let's meet there at midnight."

We strolled through the dense woods. They felt alive with activity, birds chirping, a soft wind whipping through the trees. I wondered if the forest felt the same back when Queen Catherine was alive. I could see why she liked it; it was peaceful here.

We arrived back at the dig site just as our ride was getting ready to leave.

*Good timing. I wouldn't want to be stuck on this island.*

We all climbed back into a much bigger boat this time because there were more people to transport. A lot of the diggers, including my dad, were returning to the castle. The loch had calmed a bit. That and the larger boat made the passage smoother and less gut wrenching, and I practiced my deep breathing. Four seconds in, four seconds out, just like my therapist had taught me after Mom died.

I sat with my dad and Daisy near the stern. Deacon, Remi, and Freya were in the front of the boat laughing. Well, Deacon and Freya seemed to be having fun. Remi didn't participate much. He just stared out at the loch.

I told Dad about the guards and my impressions of the dig.

"It's definitely unusual, Cat-Cat. But everyone's different. That's what makes life interesting. If we all thought the same and dressed the same and read the same books and listened to the same music ..."

"I know, life would be pretty boring. The differences are what make life interesting." I'd heard this spiel from my dad a hundred times before.

"That's right," he said with a satisfied smile.

I didn't want to listen to his usual routine again, so I jumped right in. "Dad, do you believe in magic?"

"Harley, we've been over this before. Most of what people once considered magic can now be explained by science. The great writer Arthur C. Clarke once said, 'Magic is just science that we don't understand yet.' And if you think of it that way—"

"But Dad."

"Take Native American shamans. I mean, when the Natives saw things like watches..."

"Dad."

"And, of course, during medieval times scientists and naturalists were often considered sorcerers ..."

*That explains the queen and the villagers...*

But I knew I had to rein him in.

"Dad!"

"What?"

"I know all that. We talked about it in Jamaica. But do you believe there's ever any sort of magic, any unexplainable phenomena?"

He sighed. "No, I don't. I think science has our back. If we can't explain something, it's simply because science hasn't caught up yet."

"Is that what Mom thought, too?"

I could see a little smile tug at his lips when I brought up Mom. "Not exactly. Your mom had some different ideas about history."

"I wish she was here now," I said. Dad wrapped his arm around my shoulders as we stared out at the loch.

"Me too, Harley."

~

I CHECKED my watch. 11:47 p.m. Less than fifteen minutes before I was due to meet Remi and Deacon at the stables. I padded across my room in slippers, which made no sound on the carpet.

When I moved, Daisy stirred, looking up at me. I put a finger to my lips. She gave me a sleepy look and dropped her head back to her pillow.

I looked out the window. My dad and I had rooms on the third story of the keep, and the view out across the meadow was stunning. The moon shone down like a flashlight, casting shadows all over the place. I imagined knights galloping across that field toward the drawbridge, armor shining brightly.

*This was once home to a princess, I'm sure.*

Remi had slipped me a hand-drawn map showing how to get from my room to the stables before we all parted. I pulled it out. His cartoony scrawl was a little hard to decipher, but it gave me the general idea.

"We better get going," I said to Daisy.

Once she saw I had pulled out her leash, she went from sleepy to fully awake in about two seconds. Daisy loved her walks, even if it was the middle of the night.

I opened the heavy wooden door to my room and looked down the stone hallway. Every surface was built from huge slabs of granite. My slippers made no sound, but Daisy's nails clicked if she stepped off the long carpet.

Lights designed to replicate the torches of old cast a dim glow down the length of the hall. I looked both ways and stepped out. All quiet.

We made our way toward the stone staircase that led to the lobby. I figured that was safer than the elevator. I made sure Daisy followed me closely and didn't wander off. I paused occasionally to listen but heard nothing.

We came to the stairs and spiraled down them as quickly and quietly as we could. I was safe in the main body of the castle. Mr. Murdoch didn't want to put security cameras everywhere because he thought it would detract from the medieval ambience. Shields decorated the walls, and I imagined knights running up and down the steps as the castle was besieged. At the point where the stairs passed the rounded exterior wall, there were narrow, V-shaped slits in the rock through which archers could fire arrows at attackers.

So cool. I pictured myself drawing back my bow and aiming out the slot. Well, not that I'd shoot people with arrows. But if there were bull's-eyes out there, I'd be all over that.

I paused again when we hit the first floor and craned my neck to look both ways. Again, all good. I didn't see anyone, but I could hear faint noises at the far end of the hallway.

Daisy and I made our turn and headed swiftly to the castle's main entrance. I had my hand on the huge oak door when I heard, "Harley?"

I spun around and saw Freya there all dressed in black.

"Hey, Freya."

"Where are you going at this hour?"

"Oh, just taking Daisy for a walk. She woke me up to go the bathroom...It couldn't wait."

Daisy looked up at Freya and gave her a quick wag.

"With a backpack?"

"Um, yeah. That's where I keep her snacks. She gets a reward when she does her business."

"I see," said Freya, studying my face. "Well, careful out there in the dark. Castles don't have good lighting."

"Thanks, you, too. Wait, are you going somewhere?"

"No, no. Just coming back from a meeting."

"A meeting this late?"

"Just a little business with Mr. Murdoch. Went longer than expected."

"Good night, then."

"You, too."

Daisy and I walked out the front door. I stopped a second to gather myself.

*That was close.*

We trotted toward the stables. As we grew closer, I could tell we were going in the right direction—Daisy began to sniff the air. A couple minutes later the unmistakable aroma of manure hit me square in the face.

Lights glowed out from what looked like barn doors. And then I heard boots scuffing gravel. Daisy and I bolted to a big oak and tried to blend into the shadows. Behind me on the path was one of Mr. Murdoch's security guys. He still had on his black blazer. Probably coming from the same meeting Freya was at.

Daisy and I inched around the tree trunk, which must have been six feet in diameter, as he approached. He strode along as if he had someplace to be, but then he stopped and listened. I looked down at Daisy, my eyes wide. She lay down with her paw across her snout.

He glanced around, doing a quick 360. He stopped when he got to our tree and stared at it a minute.

My heart was pounding so hard in my chest, I was sure he could hear it. My hands started to sweat. I held my breath.

He put a hand to his ear and said, "Thought I heard something. But it's all quiet." And then he walked off toward the castle.

I let my breath out.

*That's a lot of security for an old castle.*

Once he was out of sight, Daisy and I sprinted to the stables, where we found Deacon and Remi waiting for us.

"You're late," said Remi.

"We were beginning to get concerned," said Deacon.

I told them about Freya, the meeting, and the goon.

Remi nodded and frowned, as if he wasn't surprised. "She's been spending a lot of time with Murdoch and his men."

"That's some serious security for a dig site," Deacon said. "I can see why S.M.A.L.L. activated us. Something's definitely up."

"Let's read that note," Remi said. "We don't want to be out here long."

# CHAPTER 6
# A HORSE'S TALE

I pulled out the note from my backpack. I handled it carefully, hearing my dad's voice in my head. *You should be wearing gloves!* I could even see his scowl.

I didn't have gloves, but I could still be careful. I smoothed out the scroll while Deacon and Remi looked over my shoulder.

The note was written in a tiny scrawl that filled every bit of the scroll, which was about the size of an index card. I imagined the queen dipping her quill into the inkwell and scratching it out as fast as possible, the villagers gathering outside with pitchforks and torches. The note read:

NAM FALCON QUIESCIT MEDIA NOCTE
ET KELPIE NATAT IN AURORA

At first, the words looked like gibberish.

"What does that mean?" Deacon said. "It's not English, so—"

"It's Latin," I said, suddenly realizing what I was staring at. "The note is written in Latin."

"Do you know what it says?" asked Deacon.

"Well..." I bit my lip. "My Latin is a bit rusty, but I'll give it a try."

I had had a Latin tutor a few years ago. I picked it up pretty quickly, but when you don't use a language regularly, it's easy to forget. I pulled out my journal and started jotting down the words. After a few minutes, I had something that resembled a sentence.

"It says 'For the falcon rests at midnight and the kelpie swims at dawn.'"

I looked up at Deacon and Remi, who were staring blankly back at me.

"Does this mean anything to either of you?"

"The queen liked riddles?" said Remi, lifting up his hands, palms out.

"Very funny," I said, rolling my eyes.

"For the falcon rests at midnight," said Deacon as he began to pace the stables.

Then I snapped my fingers. "She must mean the falcon cages. That's where the falcon rests, right?"

Deacon stopped pacing and looked at me. "I like it."

Daisy suddenly popped up from the pile of hay she had been snoozing in. She looked out a window and then back toward us.

"Someone's coming," I hissed.

I rolled the note hastily and pushed it back into my pack.

"It's one of the stable men," said Remi. "Haste ye backe!"

I didn't know what he meant, but I got the gist.

Remi, Deacon, and I crept to a back door and ran into the night.

"This is The Bruce," said Remi, reaching up and patting the horse's neck. The big brown beast nuzzled at his hand. It was the next day, and I had wolfed down my breakfast so I could meet the boys at the barn.

"Here, give him a carrot." Remi held a carrot out to me.

I took it and extended my arm toward the horse's mouth.

"Careful," Remi instructed. "Once he takes it, let go and just put your open palm underneath it. Those teeth could bite a finger right off."

*Great. That helps.*

I was already nervous, and the carrot started shaking with my hand.

I could not believe how big this creature was. I was just shy of five foot and my head barely reached the top of his shoulders. But it made sense if you considered the fact that warhorses like The Bruce would have carried a knight in a full suit of armor, complete with shield, lance and weapons.

"What's with the name 'The Bruce'? Shouldn't it just be plain old 'Bruce'?"

"He's named after the famous Scottish hero Robert the Bruce, who battled the English for Scottish sovereignty."

"Okay, why was *he* called The Bruce?"

"Because he was descended from a knight known as Robert de Bruce."

"Hmmm. Makes sense. I think you should call me The James."

"The James it is," Remi said, laughing softly.

The Bruce was the biggest warhorse by far, and he seemed pretty cramped in his quarters. "He's Mr. Murdoch's," Remi said. "But he barely rides him. The stable boys exercise him a few times a day to keep him in good form."

The horse happily ate the carrot and rubbed his hairy nostrils on my palm when he was done. Daisy pawed at my leg. I think she was a little jealous.

Remi was giving me a tour of castle operations, hoping to spark our next clue. I wanted to see the horses and especially the falcons. So, we were back at the site of last night's close call. I looked over at the small doorway we'd scrambled out of in the dark.

"There's definitely something suspicious going on here," I said.

Remi nodded. "Yeah, we need to be cautious. I think this may be bigger than we were expecting."

We stayed with The Bruce for a few minutes, and then Remi showed me around the rest of the stables. The castle had about twenty horses in all, housed in what turned out to be a long, stone barn. I had only seen a small section last night. It looked as old as the castle itself, with massive beams held atop huge stone slabs. Hay seemed to flow out of every corner.

We walked to the far end of the stables. A white horse, like the one Queen Catherine rode in the tapestry, neighed at us as we neared her. I assumed it was a her from her slightly smaller stature and regal bearing.

"That's Lady," said Remi. "She only lets Freya ride her."

*Freya seems to have a lot in common with Queen Catherine.*

I stood and admired Lady for a couple of minutes, thinking we were bonding until she snorted at me. Daisy and I both jumped back at the sound.

"See," said Remi. "She dinnae approve of anyone but Freya."

"Let's go see the falcons," I said, thinking of the queen's cryptic note. *The falcon rests at midnight.*

The castle housed its falcons in their own little barn, built in the same manner, with ancient wood on stone. However, it was way smaller than the stables and had a sloping roof at the back.

"Is this the same building the queen visited?"

"No," said Remi. "It may look old, but the mew from those days crumbled years ago. I'll show you the ruins after we check out the birds."

"Mew? Isn't that what kittens do?"

"A mew is a birdhouse. And kittens wouldn't want to be anywhere near these raptors. They'd end up as lunch."

"Ew, Remi!"

Remi gave me a mischievous grin.

I tied Daisy to a post near the door and we stepped inside. A long row of cages lined an entire wall. The falcons had their own little roosts, narrow beams on which they sat, and each cage was open at the top so they could fly around inside the wire.

"Falconry is an ancient sport," Remi said, "and used by people all over the world. It was a status symbol in China and Japan and used by warlords in Mongolia. In Europe, falcons hunted small game. And they were often used to intercept messenger pigeons, preventing enemies from communicating. We have two types of raptors here," he continued, walking through the mew like a tour guide. "Those big birds are Harris hawks. Falconers like them because they form a real social bond with their handlers. Not all birds do."

We stopped in front of a cage with two birds. One stood on top of the other's back. They were both brown and about two feet long, with rusty red feathers on their wings. They had piercing eyes and hooked yellow beaks.

"Umm, what's that about?"

"Harris hawks are known for 'stacking,' or sharing the same perch. Sometimes several birds will stand on top of each other."

"And why are they called falcons if they're hawks?"

"It's a general term. Falconry and hawking are synonymous. Sometimes the birds are hawks—Harris and red-tail are common.

Sometimes they're eagles, and sometimes they're falcons, like these down here."

Remi pointed to a cage with a much smaller grayish bird in it. The raptor spun its head on its neck and looked at me. Like really looked at me. It leaned forward and stared at me with eyes that appeared golden.

"That's a merlin—a kind of falcon. She likes you. Female falconers often used merlins because they're a little smaller and weigh less on the arm. She can tell you're a female."

Remi explained to me that falcons were the world's fastest birds. Peregrine falcons could hit speeds of more than two hundred miles per hour when they dove, and they struck their prey like a missile. Merlins were much smaller but they, too, were fast and deadly.

"So, Queen Catherine would have had a merlin?"

"Most certainly. Not only were they more common with women but they were fierce and very intelligent, qualities that would have endeared them to the queen."

"She does look smart," I said. "Speaking of smart, you seem to know a lot about this stuff."

"Pure dead brilliant, innit?"

It took me a second to remember my Scottish phraseology. "Amazing?"

Remi chuckled. "Catching on, Harley James." He grabbed my arm and started pulling me toward the door. As we were leaving, the merlin made a high-pitched shriek at me. It sounded like the horse's whinny but much sharper.

"She definitely likes you," Remi said.

"Hey, Remi." The voice came from behind us.

A tall, brown-haired guy I would guess was about college age stood there.

"Oh, hey, Jack," said Remi. "Harley, this is Jack, he's the

falcon handler. Jack, Harley is here with her dad, who's a famous archaeologist."

"Pleased to meet you, Harley," Jack said, extending his hand.

"You, too," I said, taking his large, calloused hand. "You have a pretty neat job."

Jack beamed. "It is cool. Would you like to see one of the falcons at work?"

"You bet. Could you use her?" I asked, nodding at the merlin.

"Sure," Jack said. "She could use some fly time."

Jack opened her wire enclosure, and the merlin jumped off her perch and flew onto the gauntlet he had on his wrist.

"Follow me," he said.

Jack led us toward the door, stopping to grab what looked like a leash and something from a bucket. Over his shoulder, he explained how they'd had Gracy, the little merlin, since she was a baby. She was born in captivity, and all she'd known was life as a trained falcon.

We walked a little ways out from the mews and he waved his arm up into the air. Gracy leapt off the glove and flew about fifty yards to a nearby tree.

"We try to get the birds a lot of outside time," he said, "because they like to fly."

"Why doesn't she just fly off?" I asked.

"I guess she likes it here," he said. "Watch."

He gave a little two-note whistle, like the one I used for calling Daisy, and Gracy hopped off the branch and glided back onto his glove. Then he waved his arm back up and she went to another branch in the woods across the lawn.

"She's very well trained," I said.

"This is what she wants, what keeps her around," Jack said, reaching into the bucket. He put a squirrel on the ground and wrapped a string around its leg. He whistled again, this time tugging on the string. The squirrel appeared to move on the ground. Gracy bombed in with her talons wide and grabbed the squirrel.

"I wouldn't want to be a rodent around her," I said.

"Dead brilliant every time I see it," said Remi.

Daisy started barking from her place beside the entrance of the mews.

"I think she's jealous," I said. I looked back at her and saw Deacon leaning down to pet her. He straightened and strode toward us.

"A bit of falconry, eh?" said Deacon.

"You just missed the show," I said. I turned back to Jack. "Thank you for showing us what Gray can do."

He nodded. "My pleasure."

"Goodbye, pretty merlin," I said, giving Gracy a little wave.

She squealed at me again.

I untied Daisy, who was all wound up from the birds.

"So, off to the ruins of the original mews, then?" said Deacon.

"Yes, perhaps we'll find something to help us there," said Remi. The old mews was around the other side of the castle, and the three of us were sweating by the time we reached the site.

Large granite stones sat in a U shape. It looked like an old cellar hole only above ground.

"This is the mew where Queen Catherine used to come to be with her falcon," Remi said. "She would spend hours here, not just because she liked the birds. She had a friend in the head falconer, Henry, and she liked to escape the eyes of the villagers if only for a while."

"Friend friend?" I asked. "Like, boyfriend?"

"Some say," said Remi. "When the villagers found out, they burned this place."

We stared down at the remains of the mew.

*Remind me not to anger the locals.*

I walked around, nudging the rocks with my foot, looking for any sort of clues. Daisy sniffed around a pile of sticks in the corner, then scratched at them with her paws. She began digging furiously.

"Yeah, yeah, you like sticks," I said. "We don't have time to play."

"What are you kids doing?" A man in tall muddy boots strode toward us. "You've been poking around all morning. Gonnae no' dae that!"

I looked at Remi.

"Not going to do that."

The man was upon us.

"Remington Reid, you're always someplace you shouldnae be."

"Sorry, Mr. Angus. I was just showing Harley here around."

He looked me up and down.

"Well, don't. You ken how Mr. Murdoch is. I don't want to have to report you."

"Yes sir."

"C'mon, Daisy," I yelled. We knew when we were not wanted. Daisy continued to tear at the ground.

"Daisy!"

"Miss James, you need to control your dog..."

Mr. Angus had taken notice of Daisy digging.

"Daisy!" I shouted again.

"Or we'll have to cage her."

"Daisy!"

She finally trotted toward me, head down. She stopped halfway and looked back at the sticks. Then she looked at me. Then the sticks. Finally, she jogged over to me and Remi. I knelt to the ground and tacked on her leash.

"Come on, you," I said, giving her the eye. She dropped her head.

We started back for the castle. When we were out of earshot, I said to Remi, "Report you? Cage her? Seems a bit extreme, doesn't it?"

"Murdoch is known for his extreme ways," Deacon chimed in.

Remi looked off into the distance.

"It's been that way since Mr. Murdoch arrived. When I went off to school and came back after a few months, I was amazed at the changes. I almost didn't even recognize the castle as the same place I grew up."

"I'd hate to see what he would do with the queen's diary, if it really has the magic to control minds like they say," I said, shuddering at the thought.

"Then we need to find another clue," said Deacon. "Harley, see if you can find out anything else about the feather. We'll chat tomorrow."

I tugged at Daisy's leash as the three of us walked back to the main castle. The sun was high in the sky, and the smells of lunch cooking from the kitchen wafted toward us on the wind.

There was no way we could continue exploring today thanks to Mr. Angus. Our time to find the queen's diary was running out.

## CHAPTER 7
# THE PICKLE OF THE PICTISH RUNES

Moonlight streamed in through the window. I tossed. I turned. And I tossed again. I was supposed to be sleeping...it wasn't happening.

*Mr. Murdoch.*

*Late night meetings.*

*Security guys.*

There was too much going on in my head to sleep. Daisy lay beside me, also awake, wondering what was up with me. I sat up and fluffed the pillow, leaning back into it.

Finally I gave up. I grabbed my backpack off the floor and pulled it up next to me. I found the feather inside and began to examine it more closely, wondering how I missed the slot where Remi found the letter. I held it underneath the lamp on the bedside table. Daisy came over and put her head on my lap.

"I won't let them cage you, girl." Just hearing the words aloud made me angry. "We're going to find out what all this is about." Daisy nudged my arm with her nose and gave me a little lick.

I rolled the feather absently between my fingers. As I did so, I noticed something else I missed. If you held it in the light just right, you could see something etched into the shaft.

I peered more closely.

Along the quill at the end of the feather was a series of symbols. Some looked familiar, but I couldn't place them in my head. The sequence started with a falcon and ended with a symbol I didn't recognize.

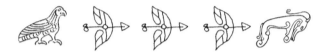

*What does that mean?*

I reached over to the bedside table for my tablet and hit the power switch. It glowed to life. I rolled onto my belly and raised myself up on my elbows. I typed in "Scottish runes." My search engine came back with more than half a million results.

I clicked over to the image button and scrolled down. First up were Norse runes. The Vikings, of course, pillaged and plundered all over the place up here. Their symbols involved a lot of lines. The ones on the feather were more circular. I eliminated the Norse.

Next up were Celtic runes. They looked extremely similar to those of the Vikings. I knew from school that the Celts were a group of European tribes that were prominent in Ireland and the UK. However, their influence stretched much farther.

*Apparently, the Celts went to the same school as the Vikings.*

Not the Celts. I noticed that the Anglo-Saxons' symbology was also remarkably similar to their neighbors the Celts and the Vikings. It was very simple with lots of straight lines at angles from one another. They were a Germanic people who crossed the

North Sea into England and set up camp for much of the Dark Ages.

The runes of the Druids, a pagan order, bore a dramatic resemblance, too.

*Wow, plagiarism sure was popular in Scotland.*

"Not getting anywhere, Daisy, they all look the same."

Finally, I clicked on the button that said "Picts." I thought maybe they misspelled pic, as in picture. But there, staring back at me, were curvy runes just like those on the feather.

I discovered that the Picts were an ancient tribe who lived in the north of Great Britain. Recorded history picked them up in the Middle Ages, but many historians believed they dated back to the Roman period. Until the early twentieth century, they were thought to be a lost tribe. And while many details about their lives and ways remain a mystery, they're considered "found" now.

"This is definitely Pictish, Daisy."

A knock on my door brought me out of my study. "Yeah?" I said.

"Can I come in, Cat-Cat?"

"Sure," I said, sliding the feather under the pillow behind me.

My dad poked his head around the door. "Just wanted to tuck you in, see how you're doing," he said, sitting on the edge of the bed.

"I'm okay."

"Pretty cool place, huh?"

"It's neat staying in an old castle," I said. "And I like Remi and Deacon."

"They seem like nice kids. I was surprised to see Deacon again. That Remi seems a little sour, though."

"Remi's fine when you get to know him," I said.

"Hey, guess what?"

"Hmmm?"

"My laptop was returned to me. The manager said someone dropped it off at the front desk of the castle."

"Who?"

"They don't know. It was returned anonymously." He furrowed his brow. "I don't get it, Cat-Cat. All it has on it is my research. Nothing personal. No access to my bank accounts or anything anyone would want."

"Well, your research is pretty important," I said. "Had you uploaded your research from the island yet?"

"Not really. We're just getting started. There is no sign of the falcon feather or the queen's diary or any of that other stuff Murdoch keeps going about."

I sat quietly. I didn't like keeping anything from my dad, but it was too early to let him know about the feather. I squirmed under the covers. I felt awful, just like I did in Guatemala and Jamaica when I had to keep information from my dad for, well, for S.M.A.L.L. and the good of the universe.

"Do you have any idea who it might have been that took it?"

"Not really, though I've seen Mr. Murdoch's security force around my office a couple times."

"Hmmm. I wonder about them, too."

We sat without speaking for a moment. My dad patted Daisy. I studied the quilt on my bed, not sure what to say. Then it occurred to me.

"Hey, do you know anything about the Picts?"

"The Picts? Well, sure. A tribe—or maybe a group of tribes—from this area. Scholars still have a lot to learn about them. They're mentioned in some of the classics, like Bede, and it's generally agreed that their name comes from the Romans. It might come from a Latin term referencing the fact that they painted their skin."

"Hmmm."

"Yeah, and they left behind a lot of cool ruins and runes, which, of course, fascinate us archaeologists." He paused. "Why?"

"I was just studying up on some of the history of Scotland."

"That's my girl. Always digging into the local cultures. Just don't go in as deep as you did in Jamaica, please. I don't want to spend more nights at the hospital."

That was in the old pirate city of Port Royal, where Daisy and I almost drowned trying to prevent a small pearl from making it to shore. It's a long story.

"I don't want to spend any more nights at the hospital either. Or at the vet, right, Daisy?"

She popped her head up from the pillow. I'm sure she didn't appreciate the word *vet*.

"Well, kid, you need to get some rest. Don't forget there's a big party tomorrow night."

"Party?"

"Yeah, they have a big bonfire every year to commemorate the Highland Games here in Scotland. I guess Murdoch does it up good with a dance, a banquet, and fireworks. He invites everyone within a hundred miles."

I laid my head back on my pillow.

"Okay, then. If there's a big party, I better get some sleep."

*A party? Why does Murdoch feel like celebrating?*

## CHAPTER 8
# BAGPIPES OVER THE MOUNTAINS

It was Daisy's howling that woke me.

*What in the world?*

Then the unmistakable sound of bagpipes filled my room. It appeared to be coming from the grass down below, but it was so loud it sounded like the piper was in the hall. I always loved the beautiful, wheezy sound of bagpipes, but it was a little early for my taste.

Daisy was wailing along with them. I couldn't tell if the sound upset her or if she was just trying to sing along.

"You okay, girl?" She stopped a moment, and I patted her head. Then she started right back up again, her snout pointed toward the ceiling.

*Is there a funeral? Where I come from, bagpipes are for funerals.*

Sunlight streamed in through the one window into my room. I rubbed my eyes and looked at the clock.

A red 9:00 a.m. blinked back at me.

"Daisy, I gotta go! I was supposed to be at the stables at nine!"

Daisy stopped her crooning and looked at me.

I overslept. The swirling thoughts of last night kept me up until the wee hours, as they'd say here in Scotland. It was at least 2:30 a.m. by the time my eyes closed for the last time.

I jumped out of bed and ran around getting dressed and gathering my stuff. I was almost out the door when I remembered the falcon feather stuffed under my pillow. I ran back for it and had just placed it in my bag when I almost crashed into my dad.

"Whoa, where are you rushing off to?" he said, steadying himself against a wall.

"Remi and Deacon were going to show me around some more. I was supposed to meet them five minutes ago. Oh." I had a thought. "Can you watch Daisy for a while?" I didn't want the dog getting in trouble and being put in a cage.

"Okay. Be careful. Sure, I can watch Daisy." He kissed my forehead. As I was hauling open the huge oak door, he turned back to me. "And Harley?"

"Yeah, Dad?"

"Please try to avoid any, you know, international incidents?"

"I will."

"And don't forget about the big party. Sounds like it should be fun."

"Right." I snapped my fingers at him. "Big party."

I RAN TO THE STABLES, where the boys waited outside. Remi was looking at his watch. Deacon was watching a falcon soar overhead.

"You're late," Remi said as I trotted up. "And there's been big doin's."

"Sorry, overslept," I said, huffing and puffing from my run. "What kind of big doings?"

"Freya accidentally let it slip this morning that they believe they have found the location of the diary."

I felt a lump form in my throat.

"We can't let that happen!" I cried, startling the horses. They looked up at me from their stalls. "Wait, my dad told me last night they haven't found anything promising yet."

Remi shrugged. "Just telling you what I heard."

*Something's not adding up.*

"I found something last night," I said. "Here, come see."

We stepped back into our favorite corner of the stables. It was beginning to feel like our own little office for S.M.A.L.L.

I rested my purple backpack on a hay bale and pulled out the feather. Then I turned on the flashlight of my phone.

"Look," I said, shining the light at the symbols. "I know they're Pictish, but I can't figure out exactly what they mean."

The boys crowded around me to have a closer look at the symbols.

"Those are definitely Pictish," said Deacon, studying the quill closely. "I recognize them from history class."

Remi almost bumped heads with Deacon as the two leaned down to look.

"I looked them up last night," I said, rubbing my fingers over the carvings. "The explanation is pretty simple. It means falcon, arrow, arrow, arrow...but I couldn't figure out the last one."

"That's a kelpie, a mythical water horse," said Remi. "In Scottish legend they can shape-shift into human form."

*Why would the queen be interested in legendary water horses?*

Then it came to me.

*Horse with no legs, just like the key to the falcon feather.*

"It seems like it would have something to do with the note we found inside the feather, but what I don't know is how they are connected."

Remi nodded. "I actually recognize some of those symbols from markers on the property. This one," he pointed at the swirly bird that looked like a falcon, "is carved into the wall at the old mews."

"What if…" I started to say, jumping with excitement. My feet kicked up straw, sending it every which way. The horses bobbed their heads in my direction.

"What if…" I said again, striding faster now.

"What if what!" said Remi. "Mon noo!"

"Mon noo?"

"C'mon now," said Deacon. "Out with it."

"I'm glad I have you around to translate," I laughed.

"Mon noo," Remi said again.

"What if it's not a message but a map? Start with the falcon, follow the arrows, and then you'll find the kelpie… and the queen's diary!"

"Like a treasure map?" said Remi.

"Exactly!"

"Good thinking," said Deacon. "You're really shaping up to be quite the S.M.A.L.L. agent."

I looked at the ground, feeling my cheeks blush.

"Remi, can you take us to the other markings?" asked Deacon.

"Aye, but it will take some time. Some of them are miles away, at the far edges of Murdoch's land."

"The queen did like her horse," I said.

"Great idea," said Deacon. "We can take horses."

Remi looked at me. "Do you ken how to ride, Harley?"

I shrugged. "I've ridden a few times. I can manage."

Deacon smiled. "She can manage." And then he laughed.

*I'll show him.*

~

"ME? ON THE BRUCE?"

Remi chuckled, holding the step stool at the huge war horse's side. "He's actually the best trained and therefore the easiest to ride," he said. "Mr. Murdoch is not a very good horseman, so The Bruce has to be an easy mount."

"I thought you said he was Mr. Murdoch's prize possession."

"He's Mr. Murdoch's prize for sure, but Murdoch doesn't have time to ride him every day. The stable boys exercise him, so this won't be much different."

"Somehow I doubt Mr. Murdoch would like me galloping across the countryside on his horse."

*Mr. Murdoch definitely isn't a fan of mine.*

"He's too busy to find out."

"If you say so," I said as a knot began to twist in my stomach.

I knew we were getting close to finding the diary. I knew that I was doing my best to uphold the S.M.A.L.L. motto: Preserve. Protect, and Persevere. What I didn't know was how I was going to explain all this to Dad, after Mr. Murdoch fired him over his daughter stealing his best horse.

But we had to protect the queen's diary. I looked at the boys, who were waiting for me to move.

I stepped up onto the stool.

"Put your left foot here," Remi said, pointing to the metal triangle, "and swing your right leg over."

I put my hand on the saddle and patted The Bruce on the neck. I'd hung off the side of cliffs in Guatemala and almost drowned in Jamaica, but this was making my palms sweat. I took a few deep breaths.

"It's okay, boy," I said to The Bruce.

He didn't seem concerned at all. He glanced over his shoulder at me as if to say, "You getting on or what?"

I put my foot in the stirrup and paused. Then I took it back out and tried to steady my breathing, balancing on the top of the stool.

"Mon noo," said Remi. He threw his leg over a pretty chestnut mare. "We have to go."

Deacon was already on a small golden horse at the doorway. They both looked like they'd been riding their whole lives.

I took a deep breath and put my foot in the stirrup again. Then I swung my right leg over the top of The Bruce, and I was in the saddle. The ground looked so far away, and my sweaty palms made it hard to grab the reins. My legs were just long enough to reach the stirrups, but I had to tuck my legs into the horse's sides to stay on.

I stroked The Bruce's neck, and he snuffled at me, which I took to be a good sign.

"Someone's coming, let's go!" Deacon whispered, nodding his head at the door. He clicked his heels into the side of his horse, gave the reins a little shake, and he was off. I did the same, and The Bruce began to lumber toward the sunlight. The ground seemed even further away in the bright light of day. I swayed a little in the saddle and had to keep steadying myself with my knees. I held on to the reins with one hand and the saddle's pommel with the other. My knuckles turned white.

We started along the trail, heading for the other side of the castle. The Bruce didn't need any instruction from me. He just followed the other horses. Sweat was now seeping out of every pore in my body.

*S.M.A.L.L. better be right about this.*

I could hear the bagpipes fading behind me. Then a shout.

"Hey! You kids! Where do you think you're going!?" It sounded like Mr. Angus the stable master, but I was afraid if I turned around to look I might fall off the horse.

Remi turned in the saddle and said, "Let's go!"

He forced his horse into a canter. Deacon followed suit. The Bruce slammed forward to keep pace, beginning to run beneath me. If I wasn't desperately hanging on to the pommel, I would have somersaulted off his back.

We flew down the trail, and I could hear several voices shouting behind us. I gripped the saddle knob even harder and leaned into The Bruce's neck. I could see the muscles in his shoulders working as he tried to catch the other horses.

We were headed toward the old mews, but I was a little worried we wouldn't be arriving alone.

# CHAPTER 9
# SCAVENGER HUNT

The Bruce was unfazed by everything and just trotted along. He was so strong it was unbelievable. I don't think he even felt me on his back. A knight covered in armor would seem like nothing to him.

Remi slowed our procession as we got closer to the forest, and I realized we had blown right past the old mews.

"Where are we going?" I yelled up to him.

"To the next stone marker," Remi hollered back.

Right. I had been so flustered on the horse I forgot the purpose of our ride. Hopefully Remi knew where to find the first arrow.

As we approached the dense forest, I began to relax a little. The path was too narrow for them to chase us in their golf carts.

It felt like we were gone only a few minutes before Remi stopped and hopped off the back of his horse. I couldn't see what he was looking at. Deacon dropped to the forest floor, too. I didn't want to get down because I wasn't sure how I'd get back up. I moved The Bruce closer to them and peered down over his shoulder.

"Here," said Remi, sweeping aside pine needles and oak leaves to show a piece of granite wedged into the earth like a gravestone. On it was etched an arrow, just like the engraving we'd found earlier.

"The arrow," I said, stroking The Bruce's neck. "Perhaps it's pointing to the next marker."

Deacon reached into his pocket and pulled out a small brass compass. "According to this, it's pointing west."

"Let's keep going, then," I said. "No telling how long before they come after us."

We trotted down the path, and it couldn't have been more than fifteen minutes before we came to the next marker.

"Yaldy!" I cried.

Remi looked at me, astonished.

Deacon tilted his head to the side.

"It means excitement," translated Remi.

"I've been looking up Scottish slang," I said, beaming.

"You're a belter," said Remi.

Sounded good, but I wasn't sure. He could have just as easily been poking fun at me.

Remi and Deacon again slid off their mounts and looked closely at the stone. This one was upright. The Bruce moved closer so I could see.

*Smart horse.*

I patted his neck. Then I held onto the pommel as I leaned down over his side.

The stone was up to Remi's waist. He rubbed some of the lichen off to make it easier to see. Engraved on the face was the second arrow.

"Which way?" I said, looking at Deacon. He had already pulled out his compass.

"North, toward the mountains."

"Into the hills!" I shouted and tapped The Bruce with my heels. He took off like a hotrod, almost dumping me off his backside.

Remi and Deacon laughed and jumped onto their horses. We all galloped across the meadow.

The Bruce seemed to know exactly where to go, and he was clearly having fun, holding his head high and pumping his legs. My knuckles turned white gripping the pommel, and I had a hard time catching my breath. The ground seemed so far down and flew by so fast under his pounding hooves. I half expected him to lift off into the air and fly.

I did a few deep breaths and calmed myself. My heart pounded, my hair flying out behind me. I was a little giddy, feeling the rush of the treasure hunt flooding through my veins.

Either that, or there was a lack of oxygen getting to my brain from being so high up on the horse.

*I could get used to this.*

This must have been what it was like for Queen Catherine on her famous rides. The Highlands were like an illustration in a fairytale book, full of shimmering lakes and lush green valleys.

As the ground underneath us grew steeper, we slowed to a trot. The trail was wide enough for the three of us, and it followed switchbacks up the side of a hill.

Remi called them mountains but in America these would be hills. However, they rose high enough to provide us with sweeping views of Murdoch's empire.

When we reached the mounded summit, I could see all the way back to the castle behind me and across the tops of the forest to the ocean in the distance in front of me.

Remi and Deacon rode up on either side of me. Deacon let out a soft whistle.

"Pure dead brilliant," said Remi quietly.

We all stared at the scenery for a time. The Bruce nibbled at the grass alongside the trail.

Remi and Deacon dismounted and looked around the summit for the marker. They walked over to the far side of the mound, where The Bruce couldn't go, and came back.

"I think the last stone is on the other side of those bogs," said Remi, pointing out across another meadow, this one with water pockets all through it. In the distance was a thick forest of tall trees. Beyond that the ocean pounded on rocks.

"It hasn't rained since I've been here," I said. "What's with all the puddles?"

"Those aren't puddles, that's a peat bog. They're all through Scotland," said Deacon.

"Who's Pete?"

"Not who. What's," said Remi. "Peat is an organic compound that happens when ground gets compressed over time. Plants get decomposed in waterlogged areas and pack down into a kind of unique turf. Scotland's something like one quarter peat."

"Scientists say it could be a great help to the climate because peat is a big carbon source," added Deacon. "It can absorb carbon dioxide and help the planet cool."

"Wow, you two sound like a couple of high school science teachers. Are we having a pop quiz later?"

"Very funny," said Deacon.

"We should get going," I said, and I waved my reins toward the trail. The huge horse immediately started walking that way.

*I wish Daisy were this well behaved.*

Going down was far different than climbing up. I slid toward the base of the horse's neck as he picked his way down the hillside.

I had to hold on with all my might to avoid going right over his head.

The boys were ahead of me on their horses as the trail narrowed to a single-file path that hugged the side of a cliff. The Bruce didn't seem bothered at all, his muscled shoulders steady, but I could see straight down to the bogs hundreds of feet below.

*Heights. Always with the heights.*

I had to stare off to my right, into the side of the hill, to keep from hyperventilating. I've been working on my fear of heights. In Guatemala last year, I got stuck way up on a towering Mayan temple and had to jump my way down. I made it out okay though, and today was no different.

*Breathe, Harley, breathe.*

I focused on the firm earth to the side of me. I could almost reach out and touch it. I hugged The Bruce as tightly as I could with both my knees and my arms and was fine until we came around a corner and the trail dropped off like a roller coaster. I burrowed my face in his mane to keep myself from looking and held on with everything I had.

That's when I heard the helicopter.

## CHAPTER 10
# THE GREAT CHASE

"**D**o you hear that?" I called up to Remi and Deacon. As soon as I saw their wide eyes looking past my shoulder, I had my answer.

"Quick, this way," cried Remi as he made his way down to the level part of the trail. The helicopter sounded liked it was making its way toward us in the distance, but we were hidden behind the hills for now.

"Do you think they're following us?" asked Deacon as the three of us sat on our horses just outside the tree line.

"I don't know, they don't usually fly out this far," Remi said. "Mr. Murdoch has his own private helicopter he uses to survey the land. Perhaps he's just out for an afternoon flight."

"Or perhaps he's looking for his favorite horse," I said, shifting my weight on The Bruce. "Either way, let's make sure he doesn't find us. The last marker pointed us north, so we should be getting close. Remi, have you seen anything yet?"

"If I remember correctly, there was a stone with markings just around that cluster of trees," he said, pointing to a patch of trees on the other side of the bog. "But I haven't been out this far since I was a wee lad."

"Well, let's hope you have a good memory," I said. "We've only got a few minutes before that helicopter catches up to us."

Remi squeezed the sides of his horse and made his way toward the trees. The beating blades of the helicopter were getting louder. They were definitely headed in our direction.

The horses picked their way through the shallow parts of the bog. I could tell they didn't like getting their feet wet. We were just a few feet from dry ground when I thought I saw the faint outline of a stone slab.

"There!" I cried, pointing toward the marker. Our horses picked up their pace to a canter and I held onto The Bruce as if my life depended on it.

Because, frankly, it probably did.

We arrived on top of the stone just as the helicopter was making its way over the hill. Deacon didn't even have a chance to pull out his compass. He just threw his hand in the direction of the trees.

The three of us sprinted toward the trees, taking cover in a smaller group of oaks. When we were deep enough into the forest I let out a sigh of relief.

Deacon, Remi, and I exchanged glances as we watched the helicopter circle over the very spot we had just been standing. After a few passes, they seemed to give up. The sounds of the helicopter blades beating through the air grew softer until all was silent once more.

"That was close," I said, using the edge of my T-shirt to wipe the sweat from my chin.

"You're telling me," said Deacon. "Do you think they saw us?"

"I don't know, but even if they did, they can't prove we were here," said Remi. "Deacon, did you get a good look at what direction we are going in next?"

Deacon smiled, his blue eyes twinkling in the soft forest light. "I sure did."

# CHAPTER 11
# WATERFALL BY THE SEA

"I remember this path," Remi said, tugging the reins of his horse to the right. The trail we found was narrow and followed a little stream.

We were walking slowly now, allowing our animals to rest after pushing them so hard across the bogs. Deacon had pulled out his compass and informed us we were heading west again.

The Bruce wandered over to the burbling waterway and put his head down to drink.

"You earned it, buddy," I said, stroking his neck.

We pushed on deeper into the forest. We were moving slower now, and I had time to take in the Scottish woodlands. They were so beautiful, with bright-green moss covering everything off to the side of the trail and long views through the trees because there was little undergrowth.

I immediately thought of the queen riding through here. I pictured forest sprites and elves, hiding behind boulders, watching her. It felt magical. Enchanted.

*Maybe that's why they thought she was an enchantress. This place is magic.*

Ahead of me, Remi pulled up, slipping down from the saddle to look at something next to the trail. He pushed the leaf litter around with his feet and then dropped to his knees and started digging with his hands.

"I coulda sworn it was here," he said.

I looked around me for any sort of indication that this part of the trail was different from the rest.

"Why here?" I asked him. "The path looks the same here as it does everywhere else."

"No, it doesn't," he said.

"Does to me."

"Well, you somehow missed that beech, then," he said, pointing to a massive tree that seemed to have six trunks sprouting from its wide base. Branches extended out every which way. It was like its own little garden. I half expected it to start walking toward us, it looked so much like something from a storybook.

"The stone was right here. I know it was. Freya and I found it when were little."

He knelt at the ground.

"Look, you can see the depression where it was."

Deacon nodded. "Maybe Murdoch took it."

Remi scrunched up his face. "Possible, I suppose."

"Are you sure it was a kelpie? Like the one we found on the feather?"

He saddled back up. "I'm not sure, but there was a stone here."

I felt my heart drop to my stomach. "Now what?"

I had risked so much to get to this point, hiding the silver feather from my father, sneaking around the castle grounds, and now I'd stolen a horse.

All to hit a dead end. So much for a treasure hunt.

The Bruce began to snort and shake his head. Perhaps he sensed my disappointment. I looked over at Deacon and Remi, who were gazing around the forest.

"Do you hear that?" asked Deacon. I held my breath so I could listen. All I could hear was the birds chirping in the trees.

"It's water," he said, answering his own question.

*Water, of course!*

"And where there is water, there are kelpies!" I said, feeling my energy coming back to me.

Deacon gave his horse a nudge with his heels and starting heading west again. Remi and I followed.

WE'D GONE another half hour or so when the stream next to us started to get louder. It widened out and rushed over big stones, forming little cascades.

"I don't remember this at all," said Remi.

The trail narrowed again and started going gradually downhill, which accounted for the stream beginning to move faster. We followed it as it grew wider and wider...and then dropped over a waterfall on its way to the sea.

The sight took my breath away.

It was like a scene from an oil painting. And perfectly serene. There was even a little walkway that angled down toward the middle of the waterfall, about halfway down.

I squinted my eyes in the sun, and for a moment I thought I saw the inscription of a horse with no legs.

"Kelpie," I whispered under my breath. But just as I was about to call out to Deacon and Remi, I heard something that made my stomach do a flip-flop.

The sound of helicopter blades—again.

# CHAPTER 12
# A SECRET CHAMBER

"Harley, back here!" shouted Remi. I tugged at the reins and The Bruce and I swirled around and ran back to the cover of the trees.

Deacon, Remi, and I huddled together in a tense row as we watched the helicopter dip and bob around the waterfall.

"They must still be looking for us," said Deacon. We waited a few minutes and suddenly the helicopter swooped back toward the trees and the sound disappeared.

"Hopefully, that doesn't mean that they've landed nearby," said Remi.

"Let's not wait to find out," I said, tugging The Bruce's reins toward the waterfall. "This way."

Along the shore, the trees were packed more densely, which would give us cover. I could see a trail farther down the edge of the cliff. As we went deeper into the trees, the thickets along the shore became so dense they scratched The Bruce's sides.

*Poor Bruce.*

"We can't have that, my friend," I said to him, dismounting

for the first time all day. My behind and my legs immediately objected. I walked back to the boys bowlegged. I'd been seasick before, but never horse-sick.

"Saddle sore," said Deacon, grinning.

"Happens every time I ride," said Remi.

"We have to go on foot from here," I said. "The foliage is too thick for the horses to get through."

Deacon nodded.

"We can tie them up out here," said Remi. "They'll be fine for a little bit."

We tethered the animals to trees off the trail, hoping they'd be difficult to spot, and then we jogged back toward the waterfall to hide in the bushes. It felt good to move my legs. We found a particularly dense spot near the base of the falls. It was so close that the spray from the crashing water soaked us.

And then I saw it.

"Guys, look over here." I pointed. The water curled over the edge of the falls in such a way that it left a gap behind it. A space wide enough for a person to walk into. When we drew closer, I found the stone I had seen earlier from the cliff.

The final symbol, a kelpie.

"Look!" I hollered over the roar of the waterfall.

Remi and Deacon pushed their way through the bushes until they were looking over my shoulders on either side of me.

"I've never seen that," said Remi in a hushed voice.

"And it looks like there's a walkway under the falls," I said, pointing ahead. "Follow me."

"Careful, Harley," said Deacon, drawing it out, as if saying it slowly would make me move slowly.

"I'm good," I said, stepping quickly under the falls. The air was instantly cooler. The water flowed over my head just out of my reach. I could see fish and sticks wash by. The afternoon sun shone through the cascade. It felt like being in a shower but not getting wet.

"C'mon, you guys!" I said, waving to Deacon, who had yet to step under the falls. "It's safe! Let's see where it goes." Not only did I think this was the kind of spot a queen would hide, but it also put us further out of the reach of Murdoch's men.

Deacon tentatively took a step under the water, then turned his head and looked at me.

*He's nervous.*

"It's okay, Deacon. Solid ground," I yelled, stomping my feet.

"It's not the ground I'm worried about. I'm not a great swimmer," he hollered back.

"I'm not even getting wet. C'mon before Murdoch's men get here!"

That spurred Deacon to action. He took another step into the watery tunnel and looked up. He waited a second. Then he started to walk toward me. Remi was right behind him.

"This is actually really cool," Deacon said. "Like being in an aquarium."

"Magical," I agreed, reaching out to touch the falling water. "Like a portal to another world."

I hustled along the path, drying my hand on my shorts. The boys eventually caught up to me. When we reached the far side of the falls, the path turned sharply—right into the hill under the waterfall. In front of us was a tall door made of huge oak slabs. Moss and vines grew down, covering its frame—probably no one had been here for a century or more. I cleared them away and grabbed the wrought-iron handle. It turned with a sharp click, and the door groaned open. Dust rained down.

The three of us gasped. "It's a secret chamber!" I said, slightly breathless.

I didn't dare step forward. Wherever the door led, it was dark as a tomb. I pulled my pack off and fished around for flashlights. I had two, so I handed one to Deacon, who was right behind me.

"What about me? Where's my torch?" said Remi.

"That's all I have. You guys are gonna have to share," I said. "Your phone?"

My light was bright enough to illuminate about half of the room, leaving everything else shrouded in darkness.

I stepped forward. The small room was no more than ten feet square. The walls were lined with various tapestries, each one a different scene from around the countryside. I placed my hand on the stone in between them, which felt cool and slightly damp. There were a few small tables, an oil lamp, and a small rocking chair.

*Where is the diary?*

Remi was staring at a long wooden table. At the far end was a black, cast-iron cauldron. "Well, that's Witch 101," he said.

"Hmmm," said Deacon.

"Yes, but look at this," I said, pointing to racks of glass and porcelain vials that sat on a nearby bench. I picked one up. It had a ribbon tied around it that read, in an ancient-looking scrawl: sage. I looked at another: thyme.

"These aren't for spooky potions," I said. "They're herbs. I think she was a naturalist or an herbalist, not a witch."

Deacon bobbed his head up and down. "That makes a whole lot of sense," he said, flipping a wet strand of hair from his face. "For the time, I mean. Strong, smart women were often thought to be witches when they were really scientists or naturalists."

"You guys go that way, and I'll go this way," I said. "We need to find the diary."

We looked everywhere. Behind wall hangings. Under benches. We moved the cauldron and poked behind the rack.

No diary.

"Look at this," Remi called. He was staring at what looked to be an old wooden bucket. "It still has water in it. What are the chances of that?"

"Odd," Deacon agreed. "If that's the queen's it should have evaporated long ago."

I walked around the room, and my foot caught on a stone, causing me to stumble.

I looked down at the floor. One of the pavers was raised higher than the others. I poked at it with my toe, and it moved ever so slightly. I reached down and tried to pull it up. It came up so easily I almost fell over backwards. In a tiny hollow underneath was a small wood box with faded colors painted in squares on each side. It looked like a medieval Rubik's cube, with sides that turned.

"What is it?" asked Remi.

"Looks like a medieval Rubik's cube," Deacon said as he walked over.

"That's just what I was thinking," I said, smiling. "Lucky for you two, I've had a lot of time to figure out how to unlock a Rubik's cube."

I picked it up and began to fiddle with it, twisting each side in turn. They moved easily, despite their age.

I solved the Rubik's cube pretty quickly when I was little, and I started to use the same patterns I used on that, forward, up, left, up. Then down, left, down, left. After I did the third sequence, down, right, down, right, I heard a tiny pop. The cube separated into two pieces in my hand.

Inside one of them was another key.

It looked just like the ones I had used on the wall of keys that was hidden inside the castle. The same one where I had found the silver feather.

*This must be another clue from Queen Catherine.*

"Guys, look!" I held it up. The end of the key had the symbol for a kelpie on it. "Let's find what it opens."

We searched everywhere, poking and prying at walls and floor stones this time.

Nothing.

"Well, we have a key," I said, trying to remain as hopeful as I could.

"To what, we don't know," laughed Deacon.

"Has to be for wherever she hid the diary," I replied, tucking it into my bag.

"We have to get the horses back before dark," Remi said. "We're already doomed."

"The party!" I said. "I promised my dad I would go!"

*Dad is going to double extra super kill me this time.*

# CHAPTER 13
# MOUNTAINS OF MUCKLE

Everything was quiet when we emerged from the trees.

No helicopters, *whew*.

The horses were just where we left them, standing beside the tree like bored kids.

"Do you think they spotted us?" said Remi. "From the helicopter, I mean."

"It's hard to say," said Deacon. "I think at the least they would have taken the horses if they came down here."

"They must have known they couldn't just strand us out here," I said. "That would be dangerous. It would take us days to get back, and it's almost dark, and we have no food or supplies."

"True," said Deacon. "And they know we'll be back eventually."

"Maybe they just wanted to know where we were going? Like, to follow us?" I said, thinking aloud.

"If they wanted to follow us, you would think they would have been a little quieter about it."

"True," I said as I hopped up onto a tree stump so I could mount the Bruce. "Or maybe they just aren't that bright."

"That seems the most likely," Deacon said. "But it is a bit odd that they'd care so much about the activities of a bunch of kids. Mr. Murdoch didn't seem to take us very seriously."

We saddled up and started to canter back to the castle.

I thought about everything that had happened up this point. The hidden hallway, the silver feather, and the rocks with the Pictish symbols carved on the side. And now we had found a hidden key...

*But to unlock what?*

We seemed to be progressing in the right direction, but we still didn't have the diary. And I was afraid we were running out of time. As I rode The Bruce, I ran through the Pictish symbols again in my head. Falcon, Arrow, Arrow, Arrow, Kelpie.

And the poem, *For the falcon rests at midnight and the kelpie swims at dawn.*

Was there something else we were missing?

A sharp sound broke through my thoughts. Deacon's horse stumbled on a rock, sending Deacon pitching off its back.

It sounded exactly like a twig breaking. He landed upright but didn't stay that way for long, crumbling to the ground as his leg buckled.

Remi was off his horse in a second. I wasn't far behind. We both ran to Deacon, who was grimacing in pain.

"I think it's broken," Deacon said.

Remi nodded. "Looks that way."

I pulled my first aid kit out of my pack and knelt beside Deacon. His ankle was already hugely swollen. I pulled out an ice pack, crushed it in my hands to activate it, and put it on the spot.

"Cold," Deacon said.

"That's the idea."

"You carry a first aid kit, Harley?" Remi asked.

I nodded.

"You're just full of surprises," Deacon said. He shifted his weight. "Ow!"

"Do you think you can make it back?" I asked.

"I don't have much of a choice," he said, his upper lip stiff. "Let's get on with it then."

We let the ice pack work for about ten minutes. I found a couple of sticks and placed them above and below the break, then tied an extra jacket I kept in my backpack tightly around them.

Remi and I helped Deacon into a standing position on his one good leg, and we pushed him up the side of his horse until he was able to climb into the saddle. He rested his broken leg on the animal's back and put the other in the stirrup.

"Should do," said Remi. "Just hang on tight."

The rest of the ride was slow and steady. We arrived just before dark.

As we lost the day's light, it became increasingly difficult to pick our way safely. Especially with Deacon just barely perched on his horse. We had to ride the last few miles using our flashlights. When we drew closer to the castle, we could see lights flashing through the sky.

*The party...*

As we neared the stables, I could hear bass pumping. Someone was playing a Celtic hip-hop hybrid.

We tried to sneak in the big barn door as quietly as we could.

"Ah, there you are," said Mr. Angus, the stable guy. "You kids are in mountains of trouble. Muckle. Muckle. Muckle."

"Muckle?"

"Big," said Remi, looking at the floor.

"Happened to him?" Mr. Angus nodded toward Deacon.

"Broke his ankle," I said.

"You two get him down and off to Dr. Perdy, she should be in the infirmary." He reached in his pockets looking for a phone. "I will take care of these horses."

"Thank you, Mr.—"

"Don't thank me yet. You'll owe me." He gestured at a bucket of manure in the corner. "And it won't be pretty."

I gulped. I had never mucked horse stalls before, but I guess there's a first time for everything.

It certainly couldn't be any worse than the lecture I was about to receive from my dad.

## CHAPTER 14
# GROUNDED

"Harley, I cannot believe it. I just can't believe it."

My dad paced, shaking his head.

"In Guatemala you stole a boat. In Jamaica you broke into a museum. And now Mr. Angus tells me you're a horse thief?" He sat down, took off his glasses, and rubbed his eyes with his palms. "You're lucky Mr. Murdoch didn't find out."

"I'm sorry—"

"Don't even start," he said. His eyes were red, and he looked like he was going to cry. It always killed me to see my dad this way. "I don't want to hear it. I don't want to talk about it. You do know your actions reflect on me and my work? For some reason, Murdoch doesn't like me, and this doesn't help at all. And I had Daisy all day." At the mention of her name, Daisy peeked out from a pile of blankets in the corner of the room.

"I'm so disappointed. And you, young lady, are grounded."

I expected as much. I was familiar with the age-old family house arrest. Part of me felt like I deserved it. I hated to let my dad down.

However, the other part of me knew what I did was right. You know how sometimes in the movies, the good guy steals the car to save the day? That's what this felt like to me. We had to find the queen's diary before Murdoch did. For the good of everyone. And with me grounded, that was going to be a lot more difficult.

My dad stormed out, leaving me alone with Daisy. She looked up at me with the saddest eyes. She always felt my feelings along with me. I patted the bed next to me. She hopped up, and I scratched her behind the ears.

"We'll figure this out, Daisy. We always do."

She stared up at me with those big eyes and thumped her tail on the bed.

*Maybe Deacon and Remi will know what to do.*

I grabbed my tablet and started a group video chat with them.

"How's your leg?" I asked Deacon.

"Dr. Perdy fixed me up pretty good, but she said I'll be in a cast for six weeks. I have to stay off my leg for the next few days."

"Bummer. I'm grounded, too."

"Me, too," said Remi.

We were all pretty deflated.

*So much for Preserve, Protect, and Persevere.*

"If the diary wasn't in her secret chamber behind the waterfall, I don't ken where it could be," said Deacon.

"That seemed like the perfect location," I agreed. "I'm surprised it wasn't there. But we did find the key. And that has to be, well, key."

Deacon chuckled, then groaned.

"The secret room led us to the feather. The feather led us to the stones. The stones led us to the waterfall. The waterfall led us to the key," said Remi.

"But where will that key lead us?" Deacon asked.

"Wait a minute," said Remi. "I should have thought of this

earlier! This castle has a bunch of hidden tunnels. You can go all the way to the stables underground. Freya and I used to play down there all the time."

Just then, I noticed a dot in the corner of my tablet. It looked like a red recording button.

"Hey, which one of you is recording this?"

"Not me," said Remi.

"Me, either," said Deacon. "Why do you ask?"

*Oh no, what if Murdoch's men are listening?*

"Um, listen, guys, I have to go. Let's chat later."

I hung up and looked at Daisy. Things were getting weirder by the minute.

# CHAPTER 15
# A LEAP OF FAITH

It didn't look *that* far down. I pulled my head back in the window. We were on the third floor of the castle. My room faced away from the front entrance, where the drawbridge was and where the party was happening, so it was dark below me.

*Everyone is at the party...*

I could sneak down and look for Remi's room, and we could go find the tunnels. They had to be the next step. It made perfect sense: the queen could travel underground to get to the stables and the falcon mews away from watchful eyes.

But first, I'd have to get down. I eyed the oak tree just outside my window. The branches almost touched the glass. Almost.

*If I could just get across to that trunk...*

Daisy looked up at me, as if to say, "You crazy?"

When I was in Guatemala, I managed to climb down the side of a very tall Mayan temple. Despite being terrified of heights. This wasn't nearly as tall, but if I fell...

Regardless of how scared I was feeling, we had to find the diary before Murdoch.

S.M.A.L.L. was counting on us. The *world* was counting on us.

If Murdoch was able to harness the power of the queen's diary and learn how to control minds? I shuddered at the idea.

I thought time was against us *before* I realized they eavesdropped on our video chat and found out our plans. Now, they knew everything we did. It was virtually a race.

I thought about the three P's, specifically the word *persevere*. And more than ever I understood. We could not give up now.

*I'll be grounded for the rest of my life. No, my dad will probably disown me. But this is the right thing to do, I know it.*

I opened the window as far as it would go and dangled one leg over the sill. If I pushed off, I could leap into the welcoming arms of the tree. From there, it was an easy scramble down to the ground. I figured the space from the safety of the castle to the safety of the thick branches at the oak trunk was about six or eight feet.

*That's nothing. I've jumped way farther before.*

Of course, it was about thirty feet to the ground if I made a mistake. Enough of a drop to break all the bones in my body. Deacon wouldn't be the only casualty of this mission.

*I wish I had some rope, just to be sure.* I bit my lip. *Think, Harley.*

Wait!

I did have some rope—Daisy's leash. It was at least twenty feet long when extended all the way out. I could loop it out around a branch as a safety precaution, the way climbers do on snowy mountains. Would it hold my weight, though? I pulled it out and yanked on it. It was about the thickness of my finger. My dad had wanted to make sure it would be stout enough to keep our precious pooch under control when she got excited.

*There are dogs heavier than me. This just might work.*

I unwound the entire length of the rope. Daisy saw me and started doing her little dance. Leash meant walk. Walk meant the best things in life.

"Sorry, girl. Not this time."

I made for the window and then paused.

Flashlight.

I dug in my bag and found my "torch," as Remi called it, and put it in my pocket. Then I crawled out the window, so that my upper half was outside, and I swung the leash like a rodeo cowboy. It arced out toward the trunk and then dropped uselessly. I reeled it back in and tried again.

Same result. *This looks way easier in the movies.*

I tried this five or six times and was just about to give up when it caught and wrapped itself around a branch as thick as my waist. I tugged. It held. I pulled as hard as I could. It held. There was about six feet of line left, and I wrapped this around my waist and tied it.

*That ought to at least slow me down if I fall.*

I climbed over the windowsill with my right leg, so that my left leg and left arm were the only things left in the building. Then I swung my left leg over and held on to the sill with both arms, so that I was looking back in at Daisy.

Her eyes were as wide as mine.

I would have to hold myself up and push off the wall with one side of my body and reach for the tree with the other. Like a monkey.

*Don't look down.*

I took a deep breath. Coiled myself like a spring.

And jumped.

My flashlight flew out of my pocket, smashing to the ground. I made it across the gap and grabbed for the nearest branch. I missed. Then I slammed into the trunk and flailed about for something to hold on to. My arms grabbed air, and I tumbled backwards. I fell through the branches, banging off one then the next, like a cartoon character. I kept swinging my arms toward them and swishing through the air. Then I was out of the thick branches and there wasn't anything between me and the ground.

*This is it.*

I saw myself hurtling toward the grass below and then, boom, I felt like I was punched in the chest. I struggled for breath—and realized I hadn't hit the ground. It was fifteen feet below me. I'd fallen a whole story before my improvised waist belt caught me under my arms. I swung there suspended. I gasped to fill my lungs. And then I rocked myself, trying to reach a branch.

It worked. Just as I grabbed it, I noticed two of Murdoch's security guys walk below me. They paused. I froze.

*Did they see my broken light on the ground?*

"You think those kids are right?"

"Makes sense, doesn't it?"

"I guess."

"We'll just let them lead us right to it."

"Should be simple. They haven't even figured out that one of them is playing for us..."

"I know, right? Could it be more obvious?"

*Wait, what did he just say?*

I wrapped my arm and a leg around the branch and clamped my hand over my mouth.

"Look at this," said one, kicking my flashlight into pieces. He scanned the area.

*Don't look up. Don't look up.*

"Yeah. One of the partygoers must have dropped their light."

My hand started to sweat. It made holding on to the branch more difficult.

Below me the guards had their heads on swivels, constantly scanning the area.

*Don't look up. Don't. Look. Up.*

"We should get going," one said. The other nodded, and they moved along into the darkness.

I let all the air out of my lungs at once. I was safe from being discovered—for now.

Now the question was, how do I get down from here? And even worse, *who is playing on Murdoch's team?*

## CHAPTER 16
# DOWN THE CELLARS WE GO

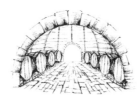

I had to tell Deacon. He was the only one I knew I could trust. Unfortunately, he was stuck in a hospital bed.

I scrambled down the oak and was relieved to find myself standing on solid ground. Same feeling I had when I stepped off a pirate ship onto the island of Jamaica, only this time the ground didn't feel like it was swaying. I ducked behind the tree to ensure no one spotted me and made a beeline for the infirmary.

Because the castle was the only "house" for miles, and now had many people on site, thanks to the dig, Murdoch created a dedicated health clinic. It was cheaper than paying to transport injured staff to Inverness.

*And if there's a real emergency, he has that ridiculous helicopter.*

I knew all this because I'd been studying the castle map that Remi had given me.

Remi. Could he possibly be working for Murdoch? He was S.M.A.L.L. I couldn't believe it. But then I had thought one of my friends in Jamaica was an agent for the Society. He ultimately was working against us. Maybe it was possible. My gut said no.

*If not Remi, then who?*

Freya? She was so nice. I liked her even more than Remi. She saved us from Murdoch's men before. I couldn't believe that either. Who else could they have been referring to?

Deacon was sitting up researching something on his laptop when I reached the infirmary. It was an old castle bedroom with a bunch of boxes of medical equipment on the floor.

Part of me imagined knights lying around groaning with blood pouring out of sword wounds.

"You okay?" I asked him.

"I'll make it. Not doing any running for a while."

"How long are they keeping you here?"

"The nurse said I can go in the morning. They're just making sure the cast sets and is not too tight. Wait, aren't you grounded?"

"This is what me grounded looks like," I said, smiling.

"Ah, yes. I remember Guatemala." He grinned and swept his red hair out of his face.

I told what I heard while hanging from the tree. As soon as he got the gist, he made the cutting motion across his throat. He reached beside the bed and took out a notebook. *They're listening, I'm sure of it*, he wrote.

I nodded and took the pen, writing, *Freya? Remi?*

He was quiet for a minute. Then wrote, *We'll have to be careful until we know. Just you and me for the rest of the mission.*

I nodded.

*Remi's grounded anyway*, he scrawled.

I nodded again.

*I'm going to go down to the cellars*, I wrote, *and start looking for the tunnels. They have to have some kind of clue.*

Deacon grabbed my arm, looked me in the eye, and started to scribble furiously in that curved-wrist, upside-down way that lefties do. *Be very careful. At every turn make sure you are not being followed. Be smart, Harley.*

I tapped my S.M.A.L.L. medallion and nodded.

He gave me the thumbs-up.

"So, your leg is supposed to heal okay?" I said aloud.

"Yeah," he said. "They thought maybe I'd need screws or pins in there, but they're pretty sure it will heal fine on its own."

"Nothing makes you feel better than doctors who are 'pretty sure,'" I said, making quote fingers.

"I know." He chuckled.

"Well, I just wanted to see how you were doing," I said. "I should probably get back to my room."

"Here, take this." He handed me his brass compass. "You know, just in case you get lost on the way to your room."

"Right," I said, giving him a wink. "Just in case."

I LOOKED both directions when I got to the stairwell leading to the castle's cellars. No one around that I could see. Then I cupped my ear like a little satellite dish. The music was still pumping in the Great Hall and outside. The bass thumped away like a disco heartbeat.

*I'm sure the kings and queens of yore would have loved that K-pop.*

The constant pounding made it hard to detect if someone was following, but I swiveled around anyway. No one around that I could hear.

I started to descend the big, granite slab staircase. Looked dark down there. And me without a flashlight.

*Wait! My cellphone.*

I tiptoed about halfway down, waited for my eyes to adjust, and then continued. I couldn't make out much beyond the beam of my cellphone, but it definitely helped to let the pupils dilate. When I reached the cellar floor, I flattened myself against the wall and listened. Nothing.

I peeked around the corner. Nobody.

I continued down into the cellar. There were a few lamps on the wall, made to look like old torch sconces. Right in front of me was a collection of wooden casks and what appeared to be old wine bottles in ten-foot-tall racks. I picked up a bottle and hefted it. It was full. I was no wine expert, but this had to be worth a fortune. I pushed a few wine bottles back slightly, just to see if they were levers or triggers, but nothing happened.

I crept around to the back of the racks and scanned the walls for passages, doors, handles, anything that could be of interest. It was a good thing I did, too, because just then one of the castle's servers, all dressed in white, came bounding down the stairs. She was a petite woman with her dark hair up on top of her head, carrying a basket.

"Wine, wine, wine," she said. "Wine all the time. Fine wine, fine wine, wine wine..." She walked up and down the racks, looking for a particular bottle. She bounced on the balls of her feet and sang to herself. "A-ha!" she said, and began pulling all the bottles from a section and placing them into her basket.

They were right in front of my face. If I didn't duck, she'd be staring me in the eyes. I slid down as quietly as I could. It felt like my heart jumped into my head, it was pounding so loud. I held my breath and waited. Luckily, she was so wrapped up in her singing she missed me entirely. Oblivious. When she'd collected as many bottles as she could carry, she walked back toward the stairs. Much slower this time.

I didn't move again until she hit the top step.

I let out a big breath.

*That was a close one.*

I turned to get back to work, but something stopped me dead in my tracks.

A hand clamped over my mouth.

## CHAPTER 17
# WHO CAN YOU TRUST?

I struggled against the grip.

"Ssshhhhh."

I lifted my left leg to kick my attacker in the shin.

"Harley, it's me."

I recognized Remi's voice.

"Quiet. I don't think they can hear us above all that music, but we need to be stealthy." He let me go. He looked at me, a little hurt. "Why didn't you tell me you were coming down here?" he asked. "Sorry about that, by the way." He pointed at my face. "I didn't want you to scream."

*Think quick. Why didn't I tell him?*

"I didn't want to get discovered sneaking around the castle. I'm grounded."

"Well, I could have helped you. You don't even have a flashlight."

"I had to climb out of my window. It broke."

"We can use mine."

When he switched it on, I noticed his knobby knees.

"Umm, Remi?"

"Yeah?"

"Why are you wearing a skirt?"

"It's not a skirt, it's a kilt. Traditional wear of the Scottish Highlands. I had to wear it for the party. Everyone else was wearing them, and I wanted to blend in."

"Looks like a skirt," I said.

He rolled his eyes.

"Wait, they let you go to the party?"

"My parents aren't around. Freya 'grounded' me."

I wasn't sure what my play should be. Should I try to ditch him or go along for now so I didn't let Murdoch's people know I was onto them?

Remi didn't look very evil standing there in his skirt. And I couldn't be sure it was even him the security guys were talking about.

*I like Remi. I want to trust Remi. We don't have much time. Better to play it cool for now and use his light to my advantage.*

"Shine the torch this way," I said, pushing deeper into the wine cellar. We were getting beyond the reach of the overhead bulbs and the gloom was enveloping me. Remi waved the glow of his flashlight across the walls.

"I know the tunnels are down here. Frey and I found 'em a few years ago," he said.

I had to nudge a rack of wine to get where I wanted to go. I was terrified I'd send a priceless bottle crashing to the stone—because it would be loud. I couldn't care less about Mr. Murdoch's stuff.

The rack bobbled but nothing fell. I gave it another little shove. Then I was able to squeeze past it.

"C'mon," I said to Remi.

He flattened himself against the wall and shimmied his way by the rack. Beyond it, the cellar opened up a bit. But then we hit a wall. Literally. There was no way forward.

"I know we found it in this general area," said Remi. "It has to be here."

The wall was built of bricks. Not huge medieval ones that could withstand a siege, but ordinary ones like they use in houses.

"I don't remember this at all," said Remi, patting the rust-colored blocks with the palm of his hand. The brick his hand was on tumbled to the ground on the other side of the wall. He pushed on the one beside it. It fell, too.

"This isn't a real wall at all," he said. "It must have been put here so they could add more racks for Mr. Murdoch's wine collection."

He shined his light into the dark passage beyond it. "*This* is where Freya and I went. There are all kinds of tunnels back here."

*Seems like if he was one of the bad guys, he'd know about this already.*

"I'd say they don't want anyone to know about the tunnels," I said.

Remi swept his flashlight across the walls. From where we were standing, I could see four openings, two on either side.

"Let's go," I said, pushing more bricks over and climbing through the opening. "Before they're onto us."

We made our way to the first tunnel on the left. It was narrower and darker but built the same way, with huge granite blocks that made me think of the game of Jenga.

*I wouldn't want to be down here when someone pulled one of these blocks out.*

"The stables and the mews are that way, right?" I said, pointing to the left side of the tunnel.

"Yeah," said Remi. "They're to the west of the castle."

I pulled out the compass that Deacon had given me at the infirmary. I swung it around until the needle pointed west.

"It must be this way."

I stepped closer to the doorways on the left side. Remi illuminated the edges with his light.

That's when I noticed the carvings. Pictish symbols.

"Remi, are you seeing this?"

"Wow, I never noticed those before."

The two doors facing west had small engravings above the doorway. One was the symbol for fish, the other was something I had come across during my research on the Pictish symbols.

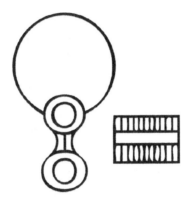

"A mirror and comb," I said, pointing to the last symbol.

"What do you think it means?" Remi asked.

"Well, from what I read on the Pictish symbols, it symbolizes wealth and status for women."

We stood for a moment in silence. We needed to pick a doorway. But which one?

*Always trust your instincts, Harley,* my mother used to tell me. I looked at the mirror and comb symbol again.

"Let's go this way," I said, starting down the first tunnel on the left.

"Why that one and not the other one?"

I took a deep breath. "This one feels right."

"Okay," he said, gesturing toward the tunnel. "Lead the way."

We started down the tunnel, Remi's light showing us only a few steps ahead. The further we got from the wine cellar the darker it became. We'd only gone about fifty feet when my notifications beeped. A text.

"It's from my dad," I told Remi. "He says I can go to the fireworks if I want. Says they're pretty spectacular."

"What are you going to do?"

"Tell him I have a headache." I typed it out and pushed send.

The screen blinked. *I can come and check on you?* he wrote.

Oh no, that was exactly the opposite of what I needed right now. My fingers bounced across the screen. *I'm just going to sleep for a bit. Don't worry, Dad. Enjoy the party.*

I held my breath while I waited for him to respond. *Okay, Cat-Cat, get some rest.*

"Whew, that was close," I said, tucking my phone back in my pocket. "I bought us some time. Let's go."

I marched deeper down the tunnel.

After we'd been walking for what seemed like forever, we reached a huge wooden door in an archway. It had a big brass handle. I turned it. It didn't move. I tried again. Wouldn't budge. Remi shone his light on it, and only then did I notice the keyhole.

"The key!" I said, fishing it out of my pocket.

I put it in and twisted. The lock clicked. I turned the handle. The door groaned open. I looked at Remi.

That's when we heard the voice at the other end of the tunnel. Someone was in the wine cellar.

And they were following us.

## CHAPTER 18
# BOOK OF SPELLS

"**Q**uick, Remi, get in here."

Remi scrambled in and we pulled the heavy oak door shut behind us. I heard the lock close in the chamber. I made a mental note to grab the key on our way out.

"That should hold them for a few minutes," I said.

The chamber was remarkably similar to the one behind the waterfall. The same tapestries, each decorated with Scottish landscape scenes. A bench with an iron cauldron. Mortars and pestles for grinding herbs. A bucket half filled with water. I peeked in. I looked up. No drips or drops I could see.

*I still don't get why that doesn't evaporate...*

This time, though, I noticed something different: paintings of falcons. There were three, and they were large portraits. Each showed the birds as they would look if they sat down for an artist the way the king and queen and other royals did.

"This place looks like it's been preserved for centuries," said

Remi. "Like someone just closed the door five hundred years ago and walked out."

"My dad would love to see this," I said almost to myself.

Remi's light played around the whole room. I studied the wall hangings, and then I moved on to the falcons. The three portraits hung above the bench, two small ones flanking a much larger one in the center. The perspective of the central picture was unusual because it was a smaller raptor, so the artist made it look bigger by coming in closer. I assumed it must have been the queen's favorite.

I stared at it closely, looking for any clues. It showed the merlin sitting on the arm of an unseen handler. She looked regal, upright, tall and proud, and her eyes showed a keen intelligence. Behind her, the castle loomed in the distance. In the foreground was a boulder. I leaned forward and studied it, getting excited.

"Remi, look at this!"

On the face of the rock was an engraving of Pictish symbols. They were the same ones—in the same order—as the ones on the feather, ending in the kelpie.

It was then I knew what the queen wanted.

"We're supposed to move the picture."

I grabbed the frame and gently lifted it from the wall. Behind it was an alcove, a little indentation in the wall. In the alcove was a wooden box.

I pulled it out and put it on the bench. It was about the size of a shoebox—the big ones that boots came in. Remi shined his light over my shoulder. The box was made of a golden wood, with the falcon symbol carved out on its top.

I held the box in my hands and used my thumbs to push up the lid. It didn't budge. As I was trying to open it, I noticed that one of the pieces of wood shifted up the slightest bit. It was a little slat in a groove. I moved it up the rest of the way. The whole box was covered in seven strips of wood, running from the top to the bottom. And they all moved.

"It's like a puzzle," I said to Remi. "They must be in a sequence. You have to move them in the right order to open the box."

I started to move them in various combinations, the way you would a padlock, but I wasn't getting anywhere. I pushed and pulled and pushed and pulled. Nothing.

I sat back and let out a long breath.

*Think, Harley. Think.*

I tried several famous algorithms that locksmiths used. Nothing.

I took some deep breaths to keep from losing my patience. Then I remembered the combination to the riddle of the feather. The horse with no legs. It was a number sequence. Minus four.

"Of course!"

I moved the fourth slat from the left. This time, the strip of wood that ran perpendicular along the bottom shifted, creating a space for one of the up and down slats to drop deeper. I moved the upper slat. Nothing. Then I moved the lower one. It created another space. I found the piece fourth from the left and moved it up this time. That created another space. At the top of the box, where that slat had been, was a button. I pushed it. It didn't open. I pushed it harder. This time it receded into the box with an audible click.

I raised the lid.

Inside sat a leather-bound book, with jewels fixed into its cover. They encircled the stitched outline of a horse coming up out of the water. A kelpie. It seemed to be emerging from the blue stones beneath it. Its shoulders looked as strong and powerful as The Bruce's, and its eyes seemed to be locked on mine.

There it was. The queen's diary.

Sought after for centuries. The object of the villagers' ire. Filled with spells. Hidden for fear it would bestow too much power to its holder. Able to control minds.

*Looks like an old book...*

"That's it!" said Remi, hopping up and down. "That's it!"

I reached in to remove it, but I stopped cold when I heard the click of the heavy oak door.

Behind me, a familiar voice said, "Thank you, Harley. You've done all the hard work for us."

# CHAPTER 19
# BETRAYAL

I swiveled around to see where the voice came from.

*Freya.*

She stood there with a smirk on her face. On either side of her were Murdoch's men. Freya's arms were crossed in front of her chest and her head tilted to the side. She just stared at us for a minute. Then she shook her head, her red hair swaying.

"Did you really think you'd find the diary and get to keep it? For a plaything?"

"Freya..." Remi started.

"Don't even bother, Rem." Freya held up her hand. "Don't care. Don't want to hear it."

Murdoch's men stood there looking intently at us.

"I can't believe you would do this," said Remi. His eyes were red, and he looked like he was about to cry. "After everything we did together."

"Oh, stop it," she said. "Don't be such a baby."

Remi glared at her. His eyes were on fire.

It all made sense. Freya, whom the archaeologists seemed to know – and fear. Freya, who did errands for Mr. Murdoch. Freya, who appeared with the golf cart and bossed the goons around. Freya, whom I met at the bottom of the stairs, coming back from a meeting with Murdoch. Freya, who disappeared for long periods.

"Freya, how did you know where we were?" I said.

"You guys were about as easy to track as footprints in the snow. But let's see. First, I stole your father's laptop. That filled me in on everything the team knew about the falcon feather and the diary. Which, funny enough, wasn't much. I thought your dad was supposed to be some world-famous archaeologist." She shook her head again and then continued. "But I quickly discovered you guys were where the action was. You're good, Harley. I'm just better."

"You're just ruthless. Heartless," said Remi quietly.

Freya ignored him. "Then you went on your little horsey adventure. That was me up in the helicopter. You missed one marker, didn't you? I thought that would bother you, Rem," she said. "Murdoch's men here wanted to swoop down and arrest you, but I thought, what's the point? Let them do all of our work. And so, you did. Neat chamber behind the waterfall, wasn't it?"

It broke my heart to think of Murdoch's goons in the queen's sacred space.

*And here they are again.*

"You..." Remi started again.

"What, Remi? What!" Freya had the same smoke in her eyes that I'd seen in his a moment ago. This wasn't the friendly Freya I knew. This was someone completely new.

"I am trying to keep our family afloat. We have been living as peasants for generations, working for whoever owns the castle. First monarchs, then oligarchs. I don't want to be a pauper my whole life. Maybe that works for you. But our family has bills. Debts."

"That diary has power, Freya," said Remi, pointing forcefully at it. "Real power. If Murdoch gets his hands on that kind of power, it could be devastating."

"Remi, Mr. Murdoch already has real power. A, he has money. That's power. And B, that's a fairytale. Ooooh, Merlin's spells." She waved her hands in the air as she said it. "I don't believe in fairytales. That diary is a priceless antique, and everything has a price. Even this castle."

"Queen Catherine would be ashamed of you," Remi said. "You're worse than the townspeople."

"The queen has been dead for centuries. She doesn't own this castle anymore. We live in the real world with real problems. You kids wouldn't understand."

She paced back and forth in front of the box. "In the real world, money talks. Mr. Murdoch said he will forgive all our family's debts. All of them. Dad wanted to send you and me to fancy private schools, right? Ka-ching. Dad wanted to fix up the mews, right? Ka-ching. Restore the fountain? Ka-ching. And if I can deliver the diary, Murdoch will make all those bills go away. Poof, just like that." She snapped her fingers.

"He'll pay for my college education and yours, too, Remi. Maybe even give me a job when I graduate. All for finding this ridiculous book." She reached in and picked it up.

"I never thought the Freya I grew up with would be so calculating," Remi said. "So callous and—"

"Stop it," said Freya. "Just stop. It's always the same with you, Remi. Such a romantic, overly smart but ultimately not a very bright boy. We're done here. You guys can stay down here in the dungeons for a bit while we figure out what to do with you."

She turned on her heel and the two Murdoch men followed.

They slammed the heavy oak door behind them. The boom resounded down the tunnel. Dust fell from the ceiling like tiny flakes of snow. Then came the ominous clack of the lock. My heart dropped into my stomach.

In just a few minutes, Murdoch would have the diary. We had to do something, but what?

## CHAPTER 20
# NO WAY OUT

"I've got it!" I said.

Remi looked up at me, quickly wiping at his eyes. I couldn't blame him. Betrayed by his own sister.

"What?" he said quietly.

"I'm calling Deacon. He'll just have to hobble down here and let us out."

I hit my speed dial. The phone rang. And rang. And rang.

*C'mon, Deacon. C'mon.*

I let it ring for what seemed like five minutes.

"He's not picking up."

"He's probably asleep, Harley. He had a rough day." Remi's shoulders slumped. "We've all had a rough day."

"True, but someone has to stop Freya."

"There's no stopping her now. We're done. She's won."

"That's what she wants you to think, Remi."

"Harley, we're stuck in the bowels of a castle. Like Freya said, it's essentially a dungeon."

"Gimme your light," I said.

I shined the flashlight around the room. I pulled on the door handle. Ducked down to see if there was a way to insert the key from this side. I scanned the floor, pulling up the rugs to see if there was a trap door. I pulled the tapestries back to look behind them. I removed the other two paintings.

"The queen would have put an escape route anywhere she spent a lot of time," I said. "I just know it."

I pounded on the walls, listening for anything hollow. I started at the bench and went around the chamber clockwise. Tapping. I made it about two-thirds of the way before I noticed something on the floor. A circle that stretched almost to the corners of the room. Inside there were Roman numerals inscribed.

"A sundial!"

"Say what?" Remi turned his head toward me from the other side of the room.

"It's a sundial. Using light from the sun, it can tell the time of day. Kind of like a shadow clock," I said, sweeping my hand across the room. "The Egyptians invented it thousands of years ago."

"But how would the sun get down here, unless…"

"Unless there was a way to open the roof," I said.

"And how exactly do we do that?"

I stood silent, racking my brain for an answer. There were so many clues the queen had left for us. Symbols. Latin…

That's it!

"The falcon rests at midnight. The falcons rest above here, in the old mews. Midnight would be the Roman numeral XII." I directed the light at it. "Here!"

We both walked over and stared at the symbol. I got down on my hands and knees, running my finger over the inscription. I pressed down. Something clicked. Stones moved. And right before my eyes appeared a ladder carved into the wall.

"It's a ladder. And ladders have to lead somewhere."

"Of course!" said Remi. "It makes perfect sense."

"What makes sense?"

"This tunnel leads right under the mews. The queen created a direct route. People always thought she was out at the mews; she was probably down here."

"That does make sense," I said, pulling myself up the first few rungs. The chamber was so dark it was difficult to tell how high the ceiling went. I climbed up.

*Why does every adventure have to involve heights?*

I rose high enough that when I looked backed down, all I could see was darkness. It helped that I couldn't see the hard floor far below me.

*This isn't so bad.*

"Careful, Harley..."

The stone ladder was so narrow that I found in places it was hard to hold on to the rungs. I remembered something Dad once told me about climbing: Always have three points of contact. I didn't move a hand or foot until I had a good grip everywhere else.

*How tall can this room be?*

Soon, huge oak beams emerged out of the gloom above me. A floor. And right above my head was a square.

A trap door?

I shimmied up to it and braced my knees against the ladder's sides. I let go with my right hand and pushed up. It was super heavy, but it moved. I pushed harder. It cracked open and dirt fell onto my face. I could see flashes of light and hear booms and laughter and clapping.

Fireworks.

"C'mon, Remi," I hissed. "I found the way out."

## CHAPTER 21
# FIREWORKS

T he fireworks thundered overhead, shaking the ground. We emerged from the dungeon and saw we were right next to the old mews where Daisy had found the sticks. Grass had grown over the spot, so no one ever suspected it was there. Daisy's digging had weakened the ground enough that I could push the trap door open.

*Thanks, Dais, you're always there for me.*

We ran back toward the castle. That's where everything would be happening. My dad would be looking for me. Freya would be handing over the diary.

When we got close, I saw the crowd. Many residents of area towns came for the fireworks out over the loch, just the way the villagers came to hear the ding in the past. Hip-hop with pounding bass—and bagpipes—came from the sound system. A DJ wearing a kilt was pumping his fist in the air to the beat. Dozens of people, most of them also in kilts, were dancing on the lawn below the portcullis. They were all boogeying around the kelpie fountain, as if in homage to the mystical horse.

The good news was that no one was paying attention to us.

"I know a side door," said Remi, grabbing my hand.

We ran right into the big belly of Mr. McKenzie, the castle tour guide. He had on a jacket and a tie and a skirt underneath.

"Well, hello, Ms. James. Mr. Reid. Where are you fine people going in such a hurry? The party's right here."

"Hi, Mr. McKenzie," I said. "Just forgot something inside."

"Ah. Have you gotten out to see much of our fair Highlands?"

Small talk.

*Great.*

"Um, yes. I went across the loch to the island. And Remi and I ventured up into the hills."

"Yes, yes, I heard something of that." He had a twinkle in his eye.

I looked over his shoulder and saw two of Murdoch's men. One was talking into his wrist and the other began to move our way.

"Gotta go, Mr. McKenzie. Nice to see you again."

"Quite, quite."

As we turned to run, I noticed Mr. McKenzie step right into the path of our two pursuers. He did that little shuffle you do with people in the grocery store sometimes, when you're both trying to get out of each other's way. He shifted to the right, they moved the opposite direction, he hopped that way. It looked like they were dancing.

*Thanks, Mr. McKenzie. I always thought you were one of the good guys.*

Remi and I raced around the corner toward the door. When we rounded the castle, I noticed an odd green glow coming from up ahead.

*I've seen that glow before. The antique statues in Guatemala, the magic pearl in the Port Royal Harbor.*

The eerie glow reminded me of why I believed in the legends S.M.A.L.L. protected in the first place. And in this mission. Because you think with all of our science and modern technology we know how the world works. But the thing is, people have been here for thousands of years before us, and will be here for thousands of years more. And it's now my firm belief that there are ancient powers beyond our understanding.

And many of the powers must be kept a secret. Or else people like Mr. Murdoch will exploit them for their own evil desires.

As we rounded the corner, I heard Remi gasp loudly.

Lying on the ground near the door was Freya. Beside her was the diary on its spine, cracked open, with the pale light emanating from inside.

# CHAPTER 22
# WATER KELPIE

"Freya!"

Remi raced toward his sister. He knelt beside her and grabbed her wrist, looking for a pulse. I tapped the diary with my toe to close it. It slowly returned to normal, the glow retreating inside. For several moments the pages remained lit up, like someone forgot their reading light inside. And then it blinked out.

"Wake up, Frey," Remi said to his sister, shaking her slightly. "Please wake up."

He tapped her cheek. First lightly, then slightly harder, like a little slap. He sat back on his heels, looking up at me, tears streaming down his face.

"Give her a moment, Remi," I said.

He nodded slightly and sat there looking at her.

"Please, Frey."

After what seemed like forever, she opened her eyes and slowly sat up. She shook her hair free of grass.

"Remi, what are you doing? What happened? Why am I on the ground?"

"You opened the diary, Freya," I said, pointing at the tome on the ground beside her.

"I did..." she said. She sat with her hands in her lap a moment. "The last thing I remember was a voice telling me to open it. I couldn't tell if it was real or in my head. But I did. When I pulled back the cover, there was massive boom, like one of the fireworks went off in my hand. I saw a blinding light and then I passed out."

"That was no firework," Remi said. "That was the queen's diary. It was open and glowing when we found you."

She glanced around for it. Then she looked back up at us, fierce determination in her eyes. "You guys were right. It is too powerful for Murdoch." She lowered her voice to a whisper. "Much too powerful."

I snatched up the diary as she stood up, just in case. Before I trusted Freya again, I wanted to have it in my hands. I gripped it to my chest.

Murdoch's security men finally reached us. I realized it had only been a minute or two since we'd seen them. It just felt like a half hour.

"Ma'am, we saw these kids run by," said one of them. "Somehow they escaped the dungeon."

"I see that," Freya said. She pulled her shoulders back. "I have this under control. Harley here is going to give me back the diary." She tilted her head and opened her eyes wide at me.

I hated to hand it over, but I didn't see any other way out of this situation.

I stretched the diary out to Freya. She snatched it from my grip.

"Do you want us to lock them back up?" asked the second man in black.

"I see no need," said Freya. "They are powerless now with all these people around. We have what we want. Why don't you go find Mr. Murdoch and let him know we have the diary? I have more questions for these two."

"Yes, ma'am." They walked back toward the party.

"We have to find a place to hide where we can think this out," Freya said. "Murdoch will be on to us soon."

"Back to our office?" I said to Remi.

"Back to our office."

We led Freya to the stables, into our little dark corner. The hay bales were still arranged the way the Deacon and Remi and I had left them. The Bruce huffed happily when he saw me. I reached up and stroked his nose. He snuzzled my hand.

"This is where you guys figured out how to find the diary?" Freya asked. "How did you stand the smell?"

"You get used to it," I said. "Let me see the diary."

She looked at it. Then at me. Then back at it. She pursed her lips. Finally, she held it out to me.

I sat down on a bale and placed the diary on my lap. It was warm. On the cover was the kelpie staring up at me.

Right then I knew what we needed to do. The queen had been telling us all along. The kelpie was the key.

"We have to put the diary in the fountain," I said solemnly.

"Wait, what?" asked Freya.

"The queen wants us to return the diary to the water. She's been telling us all along. It must be the antidote to its power."

"What do you mean, she's been telling us?" said Remi.

"Well, the kelpie, for starters." I pointed at the cover. "The kelpie is a mythical symbol of water."

"The kelpie fountain," said Freya.

"Exactly. The waterfall. The kelpie portrait. The buckets of water. She kept them around in case she ever had to destroy the diary. But she could never bring herself to do it."

"The Pictish symbols on the feather, ending in the kelpie," said Remi.

"Yes."

"You guys have the feather?" Freya asked.

I nodded.

"Now *that* we didn't know about."

"The symbols on the feather were arranged in a sequence, right?" said Harley.

Remi nodded.

"We thought they were supposed to mark the way to the diary. But what if they are supposed to tell us what to do with the diary?"

"I think you're right, Harley."

"And remember what the note said? 'The kelpie sleeps at dawn.'"

I looked at the diary, softly glowing in my hands. I hoped my theory was right, because this might be our last chance.

## CHAPTER 23
# THE FOUNTAIN OF FIREWORKS

F reya walked straight through the dancers, clearing a path. Even though the fireworks had ended, the party continued. The bagpipe hip-hop was still slamming, echoing off the loch. A huge crowd remained on the lawn and, up on the veranda, the plaid kilts kept twirling. I only saw one person without a kilt, a dancer in a hoodie who kept looking in my direction, nodding his head to the music, shuffling awkwardly.

*Some people just don't know when to go home.*

I followed Freya, clinging tightly to the diary, Remi at my back. I didn't like all the revelers being around, in case this thing went sideways, but there wasn't much I could do about that. We were almost at the fountain now. I had to admit the people provided good cover from Murdoch and his men.

*Speaking of whom.*

"Freya." Murdoch strode across the flagstones of the veranda, two of his goons behind him. He was dressed to the nines, wearing a tuxedo with his hair slicked down on his head. "We've been looking for you. I see you've been with our young friends."

"Yes, sir," she said. "I haven't let them out of my sight."

"Good work tracking down the diary. You played this all exactly right," he said.

"Thank you, sir."

*Wait. Are we being double-crossed again? Triple-crossed?*

"Now, where is it?"

"I put it somewhere safe, sir, to bring it to you later."

"I'd like it now, Freya."

"What's she holding?" One of Murdoch's security men raised his chin in my direction.

"My journal," I said, moving toward the fountain. Murdoch's guys stepped in front, cutting me off. I noticed two others moving in behind me, hemming me in. I tried to slide to the right and slip around them. They all shifted, trying to do so without drawing attention from the crowd. The dancer with the hoodie stopped bobbing his head and stood to watch us.

"We have you, Harley," Murdoch snapped. "The time for child's games and fairytales is over. That diary is mine."

"Mr. Murdoch," said Freya. "Allow me."

"You stay where you are, Freya. The men can handle this."

The two guys in front and the two guys in back closed the distance between us. They were almost arm's length away when I had an idea. I looked over the hooded dancer.

*Well, it's now or never.*

I threw the diary through the air to the dancer in the hoodie, who had stepped closer to the fountain.

The men spun, like American football players after the ball leaves the quarterback's arm. The diary arced through the air over their outstretched hands, its jewels catching the light from the DJ's console. The hooded dancer caught it. Murdoch's men made for him, and one grabbed his sweatshirt from behind. He pivoted on one leg, hopped, and tossed the diary into the fountain.

The leather-bound tome seemed to float on the surface, hover above it even, before the waters parted and it fell. Green light exploded up from the bottom of the fountain accompanied by the loudest boom I'd ever heard. Water sprayed everywhere, like the biggest pool cannonball imaginable.

All the dancers hit the deck, as if shots had been fired, and were thoroughly soaked. Murdoch and his men ducked, too, before the billionaire stood up and raced toward the fountain.

"No, no!" he sputtered. "What have you done!" He bent over and peered into the depths. The water rocked gently, as if blown by the wind. Otherwise, the fountain appeared as it had before the party.

The diary was gone.

Murdoch turned in a rage. "You kids! You foolish kids!" The entire crowd now watched the scene unfold. The enraged billionaire started to compose himself, adjusting his tie and fixing his jacket. He looked around at all the people gathered.

*He can't do anything with the crowd here.*

I stepped so close to him I was almost on his toes. He stared down. And I glared up.

"The diary is gone. You'll never get your hands on it now," I said.

Murdoch leaned over, squinted his beady eyes, and whispered: "If I ever see you again, Harley James, you will rue the day." He looked at Freya and jabbed a finger in her direction. "And you, you and your family will pay."

"It's you who will pay, Mr. Murdoch."

We all looked around to see Mr. McKenzie striding toward him with two police officers on each side.

"You're under arrest, Mr. Murdoch, by order of the Police Service of Scotland," said one of the officers as he pulled out his handcuffs.

"On what charges?" Mr. Murdoch scoffed.

"Removing artifacts from the land and not reporting them to the Crown for one. Digging up the grave of a king without a permit for another. Shall I go on?"

"I want my lawyer present immediately. And those won't be necessary," he said, gesturing at the handcuffs.

"Sorry, sir, police procedure. Your lawyer can meet us down at the station."

We all watched in stunned silence as the two officers escorted Mr. Murdoch off the property and to a waiting police car. His goons looked at each other and back at us, and then hurried after their boss.

Mr. McKenzie winked at us and then followed.

"Wow, I didn't see that coming," I said they walked away.

"Nice work throwing me the diary," said Deacon, hobbling toward me and pulling the hood away from his face. "How'd you know it was me?"

"I saw you hopping around on one leg. You were the only dancer not actually dancing. Right height, right build, little bit of hair sticking out from your hood."

He swept the red hair out of his face and smiled.

"And I knew you would never want to miss out on all the action."

After the excitement, the crowd finally decided to call it a night. Couples and little groups wandered off in the direction of the castle and the parking area beyond.

I turned to Freya, who sat on the side of the fountain, her head in her hands.

"I can't believe I ever trusted that man."

"You wanted to do right by your family," I said, kneeling beside her. "I'm sorry about all that."

She turned to Remi. "Rem, I'm sorry about the things I said.

You don't even know..." She paused, wiping away tears. "Dad never told you about how much your school cost. And all the other debts he took on to keep us afloat. Mr. Murdoch was paying him virtually nothing."

Remi said nothing, just slowly patted her on the back. She began to cry.

After a few moments, she brushed strands of red hair away from her face and looked me in the eye. "Thanks, Harley. It doesn't excuse my behavior. I know now that doing the bidding of a man like Murdoch was not the way to solve our problems. That book was clearly too powerful. On the other hand, my family is even worse off now than we were before."

We all sat quietly. And then the thought came to me. I pulled my backpack open and reached inside. I could feel the feather in my hands. I wanted to give it back to its rightful owner. But there was also something else that occurred to me.

I bent over the fountain and stuck my hands in. The water felt slightly warm. It took me a few swipes, but I managed to find what I was looking for.

I pulled my hand out and held it out to Freya. In my palm were the silver feather and the gems from the cover of the diary.

"These ought to pay off a few debts. They belong to the castle and its people, not Mr. Murdoch."

Freya burst into tears again. This time they were tears of joy.

Remi grinned. "Harley The James. You are brilliant."

# CHAPTER 24
# NEVER SAY GOODBYE

Daisy wagged her tail and panted as I packed my bags. She was ready for our next adventure.

Me? I was on the fence. Scotland was one of the most beautiful places I'd ever been. The lush green forests, the gushing waterfalls. I could see why Queen Catherine loved it here so much.

I hoped she was resting in peace, knowing we kept her secrets hidden from the evil hands of Mr. Murdoch.

"Hey, Cat-Cat." My dad knocked on my door and poked his head around. "We need to make the train at one p.m."

"Okay, I'll be ready. I just wanted to say goodbye to a few people."

"Sure," he said, leaning down to kiss me on the forehead.

Things were still a little strained between us. I felt awful that I couldn't tell my dad what happened, the real story about what went on. I tried, but as always, he dismissed it as little girl tales. Fairy stories and legends and lore. Nothing a real scientist would concern himself with. It was just something I'd have to learn to live with.

"C'mon, Daisy."

I wheeled my luggage out of the room and closed the door behind me.

"Hullo hullo, Ms. James."

Mr. McKenzie was in the lobby with a notebook and a pen when I stepped out of the elevator.

"Heading home?"

"Yes, sir."

"Well, it was truly a pleasure to have you stay with us. We all appreciate what you did on behalf of the castle."

"What will happen to the staff here? Did Mr. Murdoch—"

Mr. McKenzie waved me into silence. "Mr. Murdoch found himself in a bit of legal trouble. He put the castle up for sale, said his business was done here."

"Really? Who will buy it?"

"Well, given a recent windfall to the Reid family, it looks like the castle will stay with family."

So, they must be using the feather and the gems to buy the castle. I couldn't believe how well everything worked out.

"Wow! That's wonderful!"

"Yes, yes. No need to go into the details. Suffice it to say, everything worked out as it should."

He had the little glimmer in his eye again. And for the first time, I noticed a gold medallion hanging around his neck.

*Wait, is that what I think it is?*

He seemed to notice my discovery and swiftly tucked the medallion back in his shirt.

Then he winked at me.

"We wish you all the best."

I responded with a little curtsy. Daisy with a wag.

When I pushed out into the sunlight, I saw Deacon sitting on the fountain. He stood when I approached.

"Sit," I said, waving my hands. "Rest your leg." I gave him a hug and sat beside him.

"Great work again, Special Agent James."

"You as well, Special Agent Hopalong."

He grinned.

"Did I ever tell you about my first mission for S.M.A.L.L.?" he said.

I shook my head.

"It was a lot like this one. Only closer to home, in England. But it revolved around a castle and a chalice that supposedly dated back to Arthur and had mystical powers."

"Coooooolll," I said.

"It was. Lots of horseback action. A couple of close calls. Another broken bone." He pointed at his wrist. "Foosh."

"Foosh?"

"First responders call that kind of injury foosh—Fell Onto Outstretched Hand."

"Ahhh," I said, chuckling.

"Anyway, this mission reminded me of that one."

"Where to now?" I asked.

"Back home, same as you. Until S.M.A.L.L. calls again."

"Hopefully, your leg will be all healed up by then."

He grinned again. "Just wanted to say goodbye."

"Goodbye, Deacon,"

"Goodbye, Agent James."

As I rolled my luggage down the cobblestone path in front of the castle, I saw a few friends waiting for me. Remi and Freya.

"We wanted to wish you safe travels, Harley The James," said Remi. "And to give you a gift."

Remi held out a small box. I took it from him.

"Go ahead and open it," said Freya.

I carefully pulled off the green silk ribbon and opened the box. Inside was a small silver bracelet. I pulled it out. There was a charm hanging from the clasp.

"A feather," I said. Tears filled my eyes.

"We wanted you to have something to remember us by," said Remi.

"And to say thank you for everything," said Freya. "The gems allowed us to—"

"Mr. McKenzie told me! I'm so happy for you!" I said, tearing up just a little.

"You've taught us all a lot. About curiosity. And strong women. And doing what's right."

I was so touched, I couldn't even speak.

"I hope you'll come back to Scotland," said Remi. "Or maybe I could go to the States." He did his best American accent. "This place is like, so cool. As you Americans say."

I laughed. "Thank you for this. It means a lot to me."

I placed the bracelet on my wrist.

"I would love to come back," I said. "This place is spectacular. Pure dead brilliant."

Remi smiled.

"Pure dead brilliant."

# ABOUT THE AUTHOR

Leah Cupps is an author, designer, entrepreneur, and self-proclaimed bookworm. She conceptualized the Harley James series with her oldest daughter, Savannah, who had developed an interest in Mayan history.

The mother & daughter duo worked together to create a new world, which became the foundation for the first Harley James series.

Leah resides in Indiana with her husband and three children. She is also the co-founder of the small family-owned publishing company Vision Forty Press.

**Did you like this book and want to help spread the word?**
It would mean a lot to me if you would leave a short review online.
Every review helps with visibility and allows me to write more books.
Thank you,
Leah Cupps

# READY FOR THE NEXT ADVENTURE TO BEGIN?

## Book 1: Harley James & the Mystery of the Mayan Kings

Will Harley find the missing Mayan statue in time to save world? Join Harley and her friends as they explore temples, escape tombs and fight off some snakes in the original Harley James adventure!

### ORDER NOW AT AMAZON.COM

## Book 2: Harley James & the Peril of the Pirates Curse

Join Harley and her friends as they swashbuckle their way through the mysteries of Port Royal, Jamaica—the famouse sunken pirate city of the Carribbean!

### ORDER NOW AT AMAZON.COM